CW00376188
October '94

ISBN 1872547 86 9

Copy Editor: Len Tetlow
Typesetter: Colin Price
Cover: Val Parker

Published by

Sherbourne Publications,
Sweeney Mountains, Oswestry,
Shropshire, SY10 9EX. UK.

Printed by APW, Newport, Shropshire TF10 7AJ.

ACKNOWLEDGEMENTS

I was very lucky to have the opportunity of working with the old time hand-orientated farm workers before and after the last war. Especially learning from the shepherds and stockmen the way of life which has been their hallmark since Biblical times, in modern conditions which mirror the early days..

I am indebted to Mr. Ronnie Durham who helped to change my lifestyle by having the faith in me by allowing my enrolment in the Wolverhampton Teacher's College for Mature Students, at the mature age of fortynine! To my tutors, Mrs. Rita Palmer and Mr. Gordon Boon my thanks for initiating and encouraging me in the intricacies of Research; and the Staff of the Shropshire County Record Office and County Library who helped me in tracing the early history of Newport.

Also the Staff of the Local Library in obtaining books not generally stocked by them. I am very grateful to the Academic Authors who have published their findings of Medieval England.

My thanks to Mr.and Mrs. Phillips, who chose me to live as several characters in six pleasurable and informative years at their Tudor Re-Creations at Kentwell Hall, Long Melford in Suffolk.

My thanks to Mr. Chris Cox and Miss Tavia Mclean for checking the text, and also my ex-colleague Gavin Goulson. To Jan Shaw and the members of the Wrekin Writers Association for their encouragement to keep writing, and especially to Dorothy McNeil who took the chance to get the book into print.

Not least, to Mary my wife who has kept body and soul together, and put up with the foibles of an aspiring author.

It may be thought strange that a man of seventy-eight should have his first fiction published. But the winter wheat has to wait for long months in the cold of the winter soil to germinate and then, when it sprouts in Spring, it is harrowed or grazed short by sheep to make it bourgeon. It is always the last of the corn crops to be harvested, and the most useful.

To my Mother

THE CAPTIVE FREE MEN

The Captive Free men is the story of a fictional family. The place in which it is set is one that the author has lived and worked in for the last 35 years. The History and Geography is authentic but has been adapted to the development of the family. The characters in the story are all, each in their own way, an amalgam of people that the author has worked with. The general theme of the four books is how the members of each generation strive to better themselves against the feudal restrictions of the time, and the women who helped their men to achieve their ambitions.

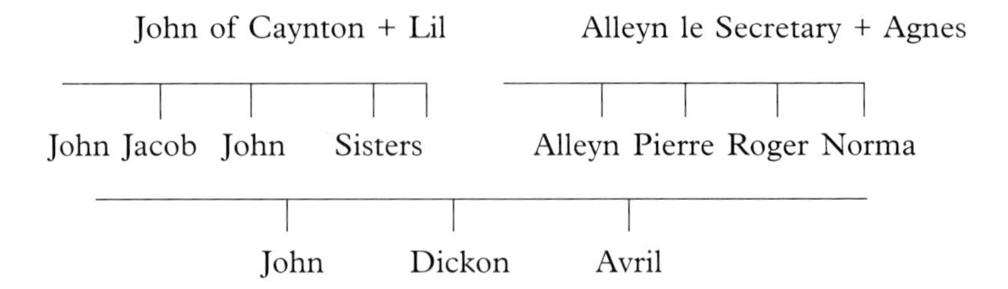

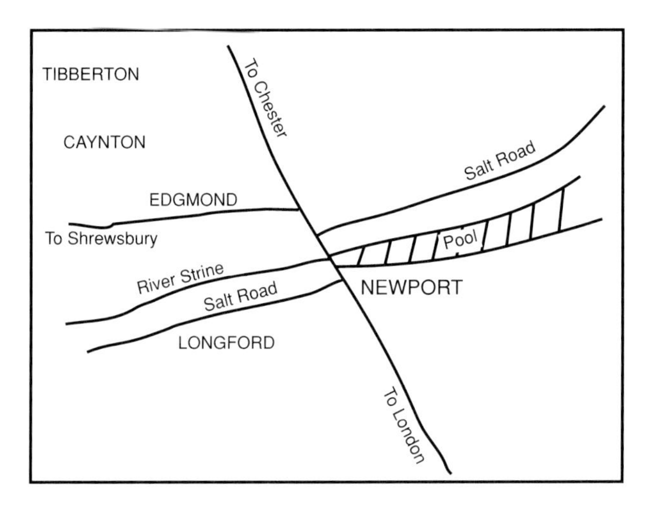

Sketch map showing roads and manors

The Plowman's Tale

By Rob Prentice

Once upon a time there were four men. They did not all live at the same time but, each in his own way, seemed to live in each other. And yet they had their own personalities, their own way of adapting to the changing times in which they lived.

Each of the men had a dream. A dream of freedom. But how could they be free, when they were tied to a dream? Married to them were the women who helped them, served them, loved them, and were part of their dream. The women who gave the men their freedom but, while they did so, tied the men to them for ever.

INTRODUCTION

The air was cool and clear with just a suggestion of a frost nip. The farmer, Mr. Marsh looked along his flat fields to the outline of the Wrekin, a hazy black cone shape in the glimmer of the rising sun. All around him were the noises of a day which had started in the darkness. He could hear a choir on the radio in the house giving voice to 'A little town in Bethlehem' while his eldest son gave a loud 'Ho up' as he clanged a metal gate open to allow the milk cows to leave the collecting yard and go back to the warm covered yard where they spent the winter months.

He limped back to the house. An exploding mine at Alamein had made a mess of his leg, but he was thankful that the medics had worked hard to save it and he could manage quite well in most situations. At this time of year it reminded him of one of the tales he had to tell. The aroma of a 'second breakfast' enveloped him as he opened the door.

"John'll be here in a minute," he said as his wife filled a cup and put it on the table.

She moved quickly but lacked the supple grace of her younger years, her shoulders bowed together with the years of constant effort as a farmer's wife.

"Kids up yet?" he asked.

She lifted her head, shrugging her shoulders in a mute signal, and smiled. He knew what she meant and nodded in response, the years melting away in their minds to when the children were the grandchildren's age.

"What do you think?" she laughed and he joined her. He guessed that they had been up since just after he had gone out to start the day's milking.

"How long will this go on," he asked, "for us I mean?"

She looked at him with a quiet and speculative glance and turned away.

"God alone knows," she said, giving him back one of his many sayings.

It had gone on a long time, ever since they were married and she had joined the family. The Christmas gathering, the fun, the opening of the presents, the tending to the needs of the animals. And then the gathering together to hear the story of how the family had started long, long ago, related by the head of the house. She had heard it all before, could nearly tell it all herself. She wondered if Norma had realised that the tradition she had started, the special feast to make the day different from the seven-days-a-week unremitting toil of animal welfare, making sure that her family would better themselves.

When she had first married, the goose was the centre of the feast with a capon for Boxing Day, hand shaped pork pies at teatime and fish jellies and blancmange with a marzipan shaped figure for each of them. A bottle of wine until the children came, then it was two. As Alleyn had said long ago, 'One for them and one for their family.' It needed more than one now, with the numbers they now had.

Looking round the kitchen at tha Aga stove and the various electrical gadgets, the washing machine and the fridge, she wondered how the lady had managed with a smoky fire and a few pots and pans. The sudden bustle of the rest of the family, stirring in the house, brought her back to the reality of the present.

Later in the evening, when she had organised the day, they all gathered round to hear another instalment of the story. She had spread the table as she had learned it, with a few modernised additions of her own. The goose had a different stuffing, out of a woman's magazine; the marzipan figures were copied from a cookery lesson she had seen on Television; the hand raised pork pies had been contracted from a local butcher, using meat that she bought from him. They had all enjoyed it and she had noticed some of the boys had 'fed themselves to bursting' as Gill had said long ago.

Her husband stroked back his white hair and raised himself to listen to the squeaky hubub of his grandchildren. His washed out blue eyes smiled in contentment as he watched his daughter, a nurse in the local hospital, who had awakened from her rest to play with them before she returned to her nightshift duties.

His youngest grandchild was at him now, putting her arms up to be lifted onto his knee. He looked at her. She was the younger son's daughter. All arms and legs, black hair and deep blue eyes, with a determined set to her mouth. A memory of one of the tales that had been handed down surfaced in his mind. He swung her up to nestle in his arms, letting her snuggle in to him and close her eyes.

His eldest grandson, fair haired and ruddy faced, a product of the local Grammar School, leant against the fire surround. A bright lad, 'going places' his teachers had said. The man was pleased to see that he had grown out of the supercilious stage and was entering into the spirit of the evening as he had done when he was younger.

"All right James?" asked his grandfather.

"I suppose so," answered the boy with a laugh.

"They'll grow up," said his grandfather, glancing at a younger boy. "Just like you have done, Will."

He had taken his usual place at his own chair by the fireside, a jar of ale to hand.

"Now what?" he asked them when they had settled.

"Last year you said that you would tell us how it all

began."

"What about it, Will? It's your turn to start it this time?"

William nodded.

"Go on then."

Will looked round the gathering and said, "Once upon a time...."

Mr. Marsh took a mouthful of ale, put the jar down and took up the tale. "Once upon a time there were four men. This is the tale of the first one. Jacob of the Marsh."

PROLOGUE

The real story began about three hundred years before Jacob was born when Earl Roger de Montgomery, a Norman Lord, was inspecting his manors in this part of Shropshire.

The sun shimmered on the close packed trees and the open moorland wastes of the North Shropshire Plain which stretched to the north of him. The Wrekin quietly brooded over the scene, as it had done since the Iron Age men had used its summit as a fort and a point to monitor the surrounding land. It had seen the Roman Legions and then the Saxon settlers and now these Norman invaders. Vinconium had been its name, before the Saxon Wreoken.

Riding on Roger's flank, one of his aides said, "With all this woodland, it is a country well suited for an ambush my lord...if the peasants wish it so."

"We have enough arms here to withstand any trouble," was the answer. "A quick change in the Lords of the Manors should forestall any uprisings, and we have the warrants to make these changes in a peacable way." A slight shrug of his shoulders implied his implicit faith in their ability to have their way if the occasion demanded it.

The party had halted on the north lip of a shallow valley, the dense tree cover on the higher ground masking the few scattered settlements. They had quit Salop the previous morning and, on their leisurely journey, the Church Clerics nominated the various Saxon settlements and noted the previous money returns which had been due to the late King Edward. Ever wary, the scurriers had reported back on the layout of the settlements together with the open land.

"Tis a place of desolation and bogs," the priests told

him, pointing to the valley. "Here and there turves have been cut for fire, but the paths through the thickets are few and there are many swamps deep enough to drown an ox. The trees are but scrub and the water courses many."

Several miles away a haze of smoke spoke of a settlement.

"What of that?" queried his Lordship.

"Tis a goodly manor, my Lord. We will be returning that way. Here, on this higher ground, is the Manor of Tibrighton."

Their journey wended between thick stands of timber and rough moorland until, at near evensong, they came upon a church. It was, in their eyes, of no outstanding consequence and the priest who greeted them of no great merit. Nevertheless the priest's bow of acknowledgment was only a token one. He knew the nominal power of the Church over these invaders of his parish.

The knights followed Lord Roger's example as he dismounted and handed his steed to the horsemen.

"Rest the horses but give the hounds a run," he said. "We tarry here this night."

As the Church bell tolled the hour of Vespers, they bared their heads and joined in the Pater Noster and Hail Mary. After the priest's blessing Sir Roger rose, straight backed, with cool unemotional eyes. He knew his place with regard to the Church but also his power over the underlings.

"Your name Father and your standing, if it please you?"

"My name is Richard de Egemond and I have charge of the souls on the manor, your Lordship, and the chapels nearby. There is an Easton Chapel across the valley and a family of monks who tend the lake."

"A lake?"

"Tis no great depth, but extensive, my Lord. The fish are much renowned."

Roger turned to his scribe. "How is its value?"

"It is one of six outliers on this manor, my Lord. The water of the pool drives a mill. In King Edward's time the manor paid ten pounds."

Roger considered the tally a full minute.

"We abide here this night. I will give it some thought."

With that he strode away, aloof, as he sometimes could be, leaving the others to make the arrangements for the camp.

His secretary and two aides, as was their wont on such occasions, followed some steps behind without intruding in his thoughts. When he came to the brow of the hill, where the land dipped sharply, he stopped to survey the scene.

Before him was an undulating landscape. Although he had no knowledge of it, he was only about two hundred feet above sea level, the valley some fifty feet below. The tardy drainage was obvious in a flat space divided by rivulets and pools where thousands of wildfowl were congregating for the night, their cries and commotion echoing in the quiet air. The goat willows, alders and rushes which filled the drier land were mixed with thorns and twisted oaks.

A wisp of smoke in the distance, and another to his left, no doubt betockened houses. He turned to his clerk.

"What of the plans for the morrow?"

"About two English miles downhill we meet a road which was used by the Romans, running South to North. That road is crossed at the settlement by a salt road from the north-west which takes to the other side of the valley, through the manors there and on to the Wrekin and the land this side of the Severn."

"Tis a beautiful marsh, full of fowl and, no doubt, fish," said his aide.

"Yes," agreed Roger, "a beautiful marsh."

He used the words 'Beau Marais', a French marque which would linger and survive for many centuries after he had passed on.

In the morning the entourage left the wagons to brake-skid down the sharp Cheney Hill and clatter over the stone dam at the west end of the lake. The harbingers, under a sergeant, had alerted the inhabitants of the settlement. The miller was standing at the mill door. Roger studied him.

"Are you bound to the manor?" he asked, using a scribe as an interpreter.

"Nay, my Lord, I be a free man working under the custom of the Manor."

Roger considered him, noting the squat dusty smocked figure and the level look in the eyes of the freeman.

"If you continue to do so," he offered, "it will be as it was." He waved the others to go on up the slight hill to the church, and examined the lake. "Is there a flow of water to suffice the mill?" he asked the miller.

"Aye my Lord....and more."

"The Salt road, what of it?"

"It doth come from there." The miller pointed. "And over the dam, and doth turn right to Longeford...as you can see."

Roger nodded and edged his horse to where a group of monks awaited him.

"You tend the fish for the manor?" he demanded.

"Yes my Lord." The eldest, hands clasped at his waist-cord inclined his head, acknowledging his superior.

"It will be as it was, now that we have taken charge. What of the church?" Roger allowed a note of scepticism to tinge his question about the wooden church beside a stone tower.

"We have many travellers..." was the defensive answer, "but we are but few souls in this outlier of the manor. We have but a chancel to house the altar in the bell tower. There is another chapel to the west along the valley."

Roger bowed his reverence in his quiet way and heeled his horse to follow the others to the settlement.

His party was dismounted, beyond the church, in a broad opening with a few houses on the rim. Most of them seemed to be organised for refreshing the passing through traffic. The sergeant of the advance party came to report.

"Tis the best ale we have tasted in this God-forsaken country. One man assays to make wine but, methinks, 'tis better left alone."

Roger laughed. "You judge a country by its food and wine, Sergeant. Mayhap, as time passes, they will learn something from us. We will have a council with my officers while you search out the way to the west."

At his council he said, "I will make this my demesne manor of Edgmondene with Reiner in charge of the lake and the fishery. Guard it well...there is money here. Thorold shall hold Chetwynd to the north of us and Longford to the west of us."

On the return journey, Wellington Manor was also claimed as a demesne manor, along with the one from Edgmond, by Roger himself. His choice of demesne manors and overseers justified his acumen. Twenty years later, when the nation wide tally was made in the Domesday Book, the return from Edgmond had risen to £15.

When he died, the son who inherited his earldom was killed in a hunting mishap, by accident or design who can say? The other brother, a rebellious malcontent who inherited the earldom, plotted against King Henry 1, the successor to William's throne. Henry brought his army to Shrewsbury to suppress the threat to his kingship and reclaimed all the lands of the earldom. Thus the Manor of Edgmond with its berewick at the lake became a demesne manor of the King.

Henry had the insight for money making and also the

power to put it into effect. In 1110 he chartered the outlier at the lake as a market town and manor. They named the town Newborough, laying the burgages out in long strips from the wide middle clearing. It thus became a demesne Manor of the King, together with, but separate from, the Edgmond Manor with its other outliers, except Adeney which had been acquired by a Monastry.

Many years later, in 1216 the King assigned the rent of the combined Manors of Edgmond and half of Newborough to Henry de Audley, a sheriff of Shropshire, on the understanding that he would 'support him in the Royal Service and during the King's pleasure.'

In 1340, James de Audley, Lord of Ruge Castille and of Helagh, held the Manor of Edgmond with its members; the Abbot of Buildwas held Adeney; the Burgesses held Newborough as a free Borough of the said James. 'And here the said James had free court, and pleas of bloodshed, and hue and cry, and gallows, warren, market and fair. And these he had used.'

Jacob's story begins two years later when John of the Caynton moor was a freeman on a virgate of land on the small Caynton Manor which had been established between the larger Edgmond and Tibberton Manors.

In his opinion, he held the land, his mother, a wife and a son. And, like the Lord of the Manor, these he had used to further his own purposes.

CHAPTER ONE

The boy, who would become known as Jacob the plowman, was born in a reed thatched cottage on a holding on the Caynton Manor. The birth was in the small hours of a summer morning in 1342.

"Lil. Ye have a man child," said her husband's mother. "A goodly lad in all faith, thanks to Our Lady." She held it for the mother to see. "He be my first grandchild."

When the cold hit him, the child struggled and kicked against the grip on his ankles. A solid slap on his rump exploded a gust out of his lungs and an inward gasp gave him his first taste of air and peat smoke. His mother took him in her arms and the warmth of her body quietened the squall of the infant, as if he recognised the bond that had united them during the last nine months.

"My firstborn," she said. "John will be pleased with that."

Her husband, a man of few words, came in from the yard outside. He reckoned that getting children was a man's job but the birthing was woman's work, so he had left them to it. He looked at the bairn and noted the well fashioned male worker for the future.

"He will be named John after me, as is the custom of our inheritance." he said.

He knew that he had been lucky to inherit the holding when he was still comparatively young. The Anglo-Saxon custom of Borough English, which was the rule in those parts at that time, was that the youngest child would inherit the farm.

When his father died he grieved not. He tried out most

of the girls in the village and settled on Lil as a wife. She had a good reputation as a worker and had been satisfactory on their visits to the bushes and therefore looked like being able to supply him with a helper on his farm, and more to come. Her father willingly paid the five shillings Merchat fine to the manor Lord of Tibberton at Wem Castle, who was losing the results of the labour of her body from his manor. By marrying a free man she was free so long as the marriage lasted. Nevertheless the freedom entailed unremitting toil, both in the house and outside with the farm chores in all weathers.

Lil was a small, raven haired, active woman who was delighted to get the chance to marry. Apart from giving her the security of a house and the status of a married woman, it saved her from the threat of a Leywrite fine to the manor lord if she was discovered giving solace to any of the unmarried fellows on the Manor.

"That was no trouble," said John's mother. "As is the way of us lower orders. Even though thou art of a small build."

Lil laughed. "I feared that it might be a big bull calf. I feel fine and will be ready for work in a day or two."

"Aye, these men expect us to be up and moving to fulfil the working obligations with no respite."

"Not all of them. My father was different."

"Thy father, had no father. Thy grandmother had to fend for herself when he went back to Wales, with the archers of the knight's company which he had come with."

"It did my father no harm. When he came to manhood, he brought up my three brothers, all good workers. And then two sisters and me, all in holy wedlock. He did say that it took a man to make a woman. So he made three."

"We'll see what you and John can make between y'."

Lil, the youngest, had grown up in a family which had

made the best of their lot. Her father was a hardworking and an astute man who used the abilities of his sons to see that they were all reasonably happy and well fed. With no great pressures, apart from her daily share of the work for her mother and outdoor seasonal work in the fields, Lil had made enough time to enjoy her youth and, by the time she was twelve years old had set her sights on learning all that was needed to fit her for a farmer's wife.

The death of John's father and the consequent reorganisation of his life was too good a chance for her to miss. She knew what she had to do, and it had not been too difficult to conceive. But, after she was settled with John, she often wondered if her ambition had been misplaced. Gone was the freedom from responsibility. The good days, bad days; long days, short days; dry days, wet days; all blended into a scheme of work which had to be done, if not always enjoyed.

John's mother, growing up with the unwritten rules which applied to women at that time, had tried to make the coming of another woman into the house as easy as possible.

"I be not used to another woman under my roof," she had told Lil. "I had three boys and a man to contend with."

"What were they like?"

"My man was easy going, but the first two boys gave John a hard time, as they knew that they were working for his inheritance."

"And they left as soon as their father died."

"Aye. They live as freemen geburs in Tibberton, with a serf's arrangement as to rent and tools. Their chattels will return to the Manor at their death."

"And John?"

"I did pander to him, as I knew that he would have the house and land. He was always a steering lad, and would have his own way. As he does now."

They knew that John regarded them both as his chattels and, after they had weighed up each others capabilities, they made little trouble. John was not a man to be gainsaid and made his wishes known in no uncertain manner. He was lord of his castle. They knew that his word was law. So did he, and acted accordingly.

Nevertheless Lil had enough sense to try and get the best out of living with another woman, not her mother, in the house. Living in John's house was a different kettle of fish from her father's home. Looking back on her own childhood, she often felt sorry for her son, but dare not show it.

John's family had never been serfs. They always had the right to go where they wished, even in Saxon times, from before the Norman Lords came. When the Caynton Manor was created they settled as freemen, giving their service as rent to the lord of the manor for their holding. They had a patch with an apple, pear and damson tree, and six strips in the common arable field. For that the father had to give as rent three days ploughing every other week in the spring and autumn and the summer fallows. Also four boon days work in the corn harvest from sunrise to sunset.

John knew that he was governed by the feudal restrictions of the customs of the manor, and knew no other life. He had been brought up to be careful and hardworking, more or less honest in his affairs. Life was hard, and hard to come by, and when he did grumble, he did naught about it. Except to rise in the morning and hope for the best, and rely on the relaxations of the Feast days and the Ploughing and Harvest Ales to brighten their existence.

In the year that the boy was born there was a famine in England and when John had paid the inheritance Heriot fine to the lord of the Manor, of his best cattle and corn, it left them short of food. However they survived, having only four mouths to feed.

Young John liked his mother who was always tried to be cheerful and, when he could walk, she encouraged him to help her in his fumbling way. She was busy all day and they were ready for bed at night, but not knowing any better he took the work as normal.

His father always had some work to do in the evening, making leather boots or leather bottles or mending harness. He bought the oxen leather ready tanned for his own strong boots but used the dead sheep fells, which he cured with alum and treated with fish oil to make softer wear for the others. They plucked the wool from the skins and his mother and Lil carded and spun the wool with the drop spindles. The second, or third, rate wool was sent to the home weaver in Tibberton to make the rough cloth which they fashioned for their clothes.

Making the wooden forks, scythe handles, rakes and other tools were another job. Too hard for the young boy to do. He tried to scrape the white beech rings for wooden plates or spoons but his father had to take over to finish them. In the dark winter nights they went to bed early to save the rush lights that they made from the pond reeds, peeled and soaked in tallow.

The only thing that the boy could remember of his first days was that the house was warm and dark, unless the door, or the wood shuttered windows, were open in the day time to let the light in. The smoke from the fire, which was pulled aside and damped down at night by order of the Norman 'couvrier feu', eddied above his head and hurt his eyes, when all the openings were shut in the wintertime.

At night he slept on a plaited straw bed with a rough hop-harlot covering. He was on the floor on one side of the fire, while his grandmother slept on the other side. It was warm and cosy, especially in the cold weather. In the morning, when the beds were stacked away, the trestle table was set up, which filled half the space. In the daytime his grandmother, when she was not working, sat on a chair by the fire, her bright eyes noting everything that went on. But the chair only took half the room taken by her bed, so she was no bother to the boy and it did not stop him moving around.

Unfortunately, unknown to the youngster, the next son who was following soon after him, was lost one frosty morning when his mother slipped on some ice when she was fetching water in a leathern bucket from the spring. While his mother was recovering from the miscarriage, John had to work under the supervision of his father who was always busy, and wanted everything done in a hurry. Young John didn't like that, and was pleased when his mother recovered enough strength to take on her duties again.

He was happier trying to work with her. Later on, when he saw the waterhens skittering across the lily leaves in the pond, it reminded him of the quick way she walked inside her long skirts. He was willing to do what she wanted, and had an instinct to do his best when she showed him how to do it. When he was big enough to go out of the house she showed him the chickens and the other animals. He seemed to be working all the time, but he felt as if he was useful. He didn't know that he was dirty and his clothes ragged. What was good enough for his father and mother, was good enough for him.

The first real trouble, which started his young mind to ask questions about his life, came one night when a strange woman arrived and there was a great deal of noise in the part of the house where his father and mother slept. The noise wakened him and he looked across at his grandmother, who seemed now to be growing old, lying on her palliasse with her eyes open. She did not seem to be disturbed by the noise, so he kept quiet and was tired enough to fall asleep again.

In the morning they told him that he had a baby brother. This pleased both his father and mother. Another male worker for his father and the satisfaction of his mother at giving him what she knew he wanted.

"Thou will now be called John Jacob," his mother told him. "Thy brother will have the name of John."

He did not understand that, and it puzzled him for a long time, as he liked having the same name as his father. He was not to know that the heir had to called John and it would happen again to his brother, if his mother had another son. But he got used to being called Jacob, and began to like it. It gave him a feeling of being special.

He began to feel irritated by the smallness of the room in the house where they spent their days. The new baby and his grandmother and his father and mother, all got in the way when he wanted to move around. Another thing to add to his frustration, he found that, now that his mother had other tasks to occupy her and did not have the time to do all her chores, he had to work again under his father's supervision.

"Thou art coming up to three years old now," his father said. "Tis high time that thou shouldst earn thy keep."

Earning his keep meant that his work load built up under his father's orders. He had been fetching in the peat turves for the fire, and gathering what sticks he could find. Now he had to feed the chickens and gather the eggs at laying time and, when he grew bigger, even goad the oxen when his father ploughed his own land. At one time he would have been proud of being able to do the tasks, but his father's gruff way of telling him to do this or that was often accompanied by a cuff on the ear if he was not quick enough to satisfy him.

To him his father seemed a mountain of a man and moved heavier objects than his mother could , which Jacob thought was wonderful. However, Jacob recovered his enthusiasm when the baby could be left with his grandmother, and his mother was able to do her share again.

He began to take more notice of the house and buildings. His father was the third generation on the holding and the house had been added to, as it was required.

The middle room, where all the cooking and eating and sleeping was done, had the fire place with the smoke rising up through the rushes in the roof. It was in a corner, out of the way, but handy for cooking. There was always some broth with peas or beans, simmering in an iron pot hung above it and his mother allowed him to have a sup whenever he felt like it. Which was quite often with the work he had to do. But Jacob was growing to the work and meant to be as big as his father as soon as he could.

The walls of the house were thick and smooth and, here and there, wooden uprights made a frame with some pegs driven in to hang things on. In the wet weather his mother covered the hammered earth floor with rushes, which she swept out with a broom and changed once a week. The rubbish had to be carried to the midden where the straw from the oxen bedding was stacked and where they went to relieve themselves in a little shed built on one side.

In the room where his father and mother slept they kept their spare clothes in a chest. His bed was stored there in the daytime and brought out again when it was his bedtime. At the other end was the building where they kept the oxen, and the chickens slept at night, although they spent some time during the day foraging in the house for any titbits on the floor.

One of the chores that his father had added for Jacob to earn his keep was to clean out the shit from the shed where the oxen slept. It would have taken his father five minutes, but he reckoned that it was Jacob's job and he left him to it. It took Jacob longer than that. He liked the oxen and often, at night, he curled up in the straw to enjoy the warmth. The musty smell soon sent him off to sleep.

They had two beasts, one that they milked night and morning. His mother showed him how to squeeze the teats and fill the milk into the bucket. As his mother was always busy it gradually became his task.

His father began to go out early in the mornings with the oxen and come back late in the afternoons, complaining to the women folks about a shortage of men on the demesne and having to spend more time than usual on the manor land with the extra ploughing. He forgot to mention that he was earning extra money as day work.

It meant that he began to grumble at everything and everybody, his heavy hand ready to fall at the slightest mistake, real or imagined. He was not a vicious man and Jacob learned that if he managed to duck the expected blow his father was not bothered and never followed it up. However he tried to keep out of his father's way when he was outside. But when he was inside the house, he felt that it was full of bodies and benches and the table.

One evening, when it had been raining all day, it became dark before his father showed up with his smock wringing wet. After he had fed the oxen, Jacob went into the house to fetch the bucket for milking. His father had taken off his smock and was standing bare chested while his mother was rubbing him down and complaining that he would catch the ague.

Jacob had never seen him like that before. A thick curly mat of golden hair covered his front and across the back of his shoulders, his skin glowing red where the rough homespun cloth had dried him. His mother knelt down to undo the laces on the wet leggings, and the separate legs of his upper hose which had come undone from his under-shirt fastenings at the waist..

His father gave a deep laugh, pulled his mother to her feet and started wrestling with her. Jacob moved to stop him but his grandmother held up her hand. After struggling a while his mother became all quiet and submitted. They stood close together until his mother turned to move away. His father held her tighter, not letting her go and bent her forward, pulling at her clothes. Jacob looked at his grandmother whose shining eyes were fixed on the couple and her toothless lips trembling while she nodded her head in agreement to his father's questioning look.

Suddenly Jacob felt that it was not the place for him but curiosity held him transfixed. His father had pulled his mother's skirts right up and was moving back and forward at her. She had given up struggling and didn't seem to mind. Suddenly he stopped, and stood back slowly, giving his mother a slap on her buttocks. John grabbed the bucket, and went out to do his milking chore.

He began to hate his mother when she had another baby, a girl this time. Another non-worker. He was a bright lad, keen and an easy learner. But now it was all changing and he was noticing the changes and didn't like them. It irked him that he didn't know how to make life any better. But, for the time being, he put up with it and tried to do his best.

Jacob began to be worried about the milk cow when he could not get as much milk from her as he should. He expected that he would get the blame for that as well, and was surprised when his father said,

"Worry not. Feed her better. There will be plenty soon. Take what you can get."

But soon she stopped giving any at all. Jacob, who knew nothing about such things, could not see anything wrong with her, but he began to sleep in the byre with the oxen just to make sure.

He had just fallen off to sleep one night when he was awakened by the cow straining on her neck halter and giving deep groans that seemed to come from her belly. He got up and lit a candle to see what was the matter. What he saw frightened the life out of him and he went to waken his father.

"The inside cometh out of the cow," he yelled to waken him.

"Worry not. Tis no mischance," he was told. "I be coming presently."

When they got to the byre his father asked, "Ye have not seen this afore?"

Jacob agreed, his eyes wide open in wonderment.

His father went to the bullock's head, undid the necktie and gave Jacob the lead rope. In his usual gruff voice he said, "here. Take this bugger, and get him out of the way."

"Where?"

"I know not. Tie him up somewhere. Tie him to a stake and go inside."

Jacob did his best to pull the beast out and keep the wide horns from catching on everything. He hunted round in the darkness to find a spot to fasten the ox with his newly learned bowline knot with the slip for an easy undoing. He pulled hard to test the surety of the hold and went back into the barn to see what was going on.

They stood in silence for a while as the cow reached back on its halter rope and gave some more deep throaty groans. To Jacob's amazement he saw two feet coming out of the cow's backside.

"Fine," said his father, "front legs. It may well be not long now. Tis her second."

He was right. The feet were followed by the rest of the legs and then the nose of the calf lying between them. The cow stopped for a breather and his father took a leg in each hand.

"Come on now lass." His voice was kindly. Jacob had never heard him speak kindly before, and would never hear again except at calving or lambing.

"Come on now," his father coaxed, tightening his shoulders and with steady, gentle strength he eased the calf out of the restricting passage. As it flopped on the floor he cleaned its nose and mouth and pulled it up to the cow to let it smell and lick it.

"Go inside now," his father said. "Tis no place here for thee this night."

"What is it?" his mother asked him when he reached the house.

"A calf."

"I know that," she said. "A heifer or a bull?"

Jacob had no idea and said so.

"Tis the first thing you find out. Tis needful that we have two cows so that we can have more calves."

She seemed to think that Jacob knew all about it.

"Where did it come from?" he asked .

"Your father put it to the Manor bull one day when he was ploughing up there." She thought that was good enough.

His mother came to help him at the milking next morning. The cow's udder had grown hard with the new milk and she showed him what to do. The milk was a dark yellow, not like the white stuff that he had been used to.

"We make some custard with this for a day or two until it clears," she told him. She had brought a leather collar which she put round the calf's neck and tied it up. Lifting it's tail she had a look. "A heifer," she said. "Keep the collar on when it be young and twill remember it for ever. Keep it away from the cow while you milk what we need, and then let it have the finishings."

It was another chore for Jacob, one which he liked. It was the first young thing that he had for himself and it became, in his mind, his own. He soon had the feeding organised, suckling the calf twice a day at milking times and giving it some heated milk at mid-day.

At night he had a shedful, the big gelded ox, the neat milk cow, and his own calf, a heifer at that.

"Some day 'twill give us some milk to keep us supplied when the other is dry," his mother explained.

It was the first of his many tasks that he did not grumble about. And his father left him to it.

'This is what I want,' he decided. 'I will be a herdsman, tending the oxen, one day.'

CHAPTER TWO

It was a hard life for Jacob. In the snow and ice of winter he wrapped himself up as best he could and kept out of his father's way, especially when he was irritated by Jacob's inability to do some of the winter jobs. His father, who was determined to get the best out of him, nevertheless had to admit that many of the farm jobs were too much for the young lad.

"I have no time to tell thee everything," he said. "But there is much to do. Use thy sense to do the best to thy strength. When the tasks have to be done, then they have to be done, whether we like it or not"

His father seemed to be made of iron, not feeling the cold on his chapped hands, the misty breath coming out of his blue nose. He was not overly keen on spending money on clothes so they got by with a rough, tufty, loose woven cloth, which was made mostly with the coarse spun yarn from the sheep fells, on a Tibberton weaver's standing loom. The women were allowed a linen smock under their cheap wool kirtle. For that they had a stand of flax at the end of the garden which supplied the yarn.

They let their hair grow long, becoming matted and itchy, rubbing their chests with goosegrease to give themselves uncomfortable warmth. When the cold reached into the house at night they would fetch in some sheep pelts to cover themselves, and put up with the stink of the dead skins.

As the snow covering showed up their footprints, poaching was a hazardous escapade, and left them to rely on what salted meat they had, and the cheese that had been made from the sheep milk, which they had been able to store. Many a day Jacob was forced to save the hard bacon rind and keep chewing it until it was soft enough to swallow. Lil would make a browis with scalded bread flavoured with butter and onions. The greens from the garden, which stood the winter frosts, and the wild garlic from the woods kept them in some sort of health.

John had been through it all before and did his best to stock up for the bad times, and Lil had her own way of seeing that her men were cared for as best she could. At least they were better off than the serfs who had no land of their own.

Suddenly the sun was shining again and the birds were singing and the turtle doves were burbling their incessant gossiping in the woods. Jacob was glad to get out and about and take notice of the changes that the season had brought. A bird was calling all day and all night as if mocking them and another was croaking away in the ploughlands. His mother too, seemed to brighten up and when the laying time came she had a chance to augment their diet with the eggs that he found.

Being on his own, with no older children to tutor him, he had to discover the different trees and birds for himself. In his expeditions into the spinneys and the larger stands of trees, he found other nests and even tried to practise setting snares for the conies which ran away when he approached them. But he had no success, and so was saved the threat of being caught poaching.

Gossip was the means of spreading news in the community, although it was not always to be relied on. He did not understand his father and mother discussing the news, which had come to them from Newborough market, about people in the Country dying in their hundreds of some terrible plague. Being well away from the busy Chester road they escaped the affliction, but he overheard his father and mother talking together one night.

"There be a great tale from Tibberton," his father was saying.

"What be that?"

"They found a packhorse the other morning, stood at the top of the hill from Adeney."

"By itself?" asked his grandmother.

"Nay. That be the tale of it. Twas standing, with the packman dead as could be."

"How could that be," asked his mother.

"He must have been clemmed with climbing the hill and laid down for a rest." His father waited a minute. "He was all marked with the plague."

"Gods a mercy!" gasped his grandmother, crossing herself.

"The Blessed Mother guard us," said his mother, doing likewise, and looking at them all with fright in her eyes.

"Tis all right," soothed John. "They rolled him into a ditch with spades and covered him. Then they cut his pack off the horse and burned it on top of the burial."

"God rest his soul," said the women, crossing themselves again.

John laughed. "Well, ponies get not the plague. So someone took it down to Newborough market and sold it. And they all shared in a drink with the money."

"We want it not here," said his mother.

"If we keep ourselves to ourselves we may be well rid of it," was his father's opinion.

Jacob, who knew naught of the plague, thought it quite a tale.

The shortage of labour in the towns, caused by the high mortality rate, had changed the opinions of some of the workers. At last there was the chance of throwing off their serf bondage. The promise of well paid jobs in the towns, coupled with the fact that, if any serf could work away from his Manor for a year and a day without being found out then he was free, had caused unrest in the rural areas.

"Two men who worked on the Manor have disappeared," he heard his father say. "A young man of marriageable age from the Caynton serfs went with an older man from Tibberton, who left his wife and family to fend for themselves."

"Our lady save us!" said his grandmother. "Where went they?"

"Tis said that they headed towards Shrewsbury. Tis the biggest town nearby."

"Out of the frying pan into the fire," was his father's opinion. "They may find the plague more to contend with."

It meant that the bailiff was driving hard trying to get the owner's demesne work done and was pressing Jacob's father to work more days for cash wages. The pay for the extra time that he put in was ready money for John but it meant that his own farm suffered, as he had to neglect the work on his own crops. It did not help his temper in any way, especially as young Jacob was not big enough to carry out many of the necessary tasks; and was too young to hire out to the demesne land if his father stopped at home.

It had been a very poor lamb crop in the manor flock and the bailiff, wanting to maintain his wool harvest, bought some ewes which he had been offered at a very cheap price at Newborough Market. His secondary thought was not only of keeping the wool producing numbers up, but also to use them to graze the land which he was not able to cultivate through lack of man power. John thought the idea was a good one to use on his own land, and also a way get some work out of

Jacob by his tending them. So he offered to take ten ewes against the wage money he was earning.

He built a pen to hold them at night and, one day, he went off without the oxen and arrived home with the sheep. He had been unable to plough all the land that he meant to and had plenty of unploughed grassed over stubble land. It meant more work for Jacob who had to shepherd them when they grazed in the day time. He still had his milking to do in the morning, and in the evening when he had penned the sheep. But his mother took care of the other work.

There was a drought that Spring and he enjoyed the good summer-like weather and being on his own, away from everybody. He had learned the sling shooting when he was scaring birds off the corn and found that it was a good idea to keep the sheep from straying.

Sometimes, when the ewes were lying down chewing the cud, the inactivity palled on him and he would go investigating the bushes, but it was too late for eggs and the birds had flown their nests. He saw a group of tall dark trees which seemed to stand out from the others but they were too far away to investigate.

"What be they?" he asked his mother. She looked surprised and then alarmed. "Thou hast not been there?" she demanded.

"Nay. Why?"

"That be Spray Hill. They be black pines....there from times of long ago. We frequent not that grove." She crossed herself, twice. "Tis a place of black priests and bugans and such like witchcrafts."

"Have ye seen them?"

"Nay. Tis all in the tales that are told in the dark winter nights, when the wind soughs through the branches like ghosts and dead spirits seeking a resting place."

He thought it strange but he kept away from the place

and concentrated his mind on the here and now. He found a few coney runs and learned the art of setting the wire snares on the runs....the sliding loop, head high to the unsuspecting quarry. His mother was delighted but warned him 'that it was not for gossip'. He did not understand what she meant at the time but, later on when he began to meet other people, he had learned how to keep his thoughts to himself.

He was getting older and stronger and the tasks were becoming easier. Sometimes he would sit, but not often, because that was when his mind would start to think; of his life and constant work; of his father whom he hated for his overbearing ways; of his mother whom he disliked when she had another baby and made more work for him; especially of the never ending work; and more especially the unspoken knowledge that one of his brothers would inherit the farm and the fruits of his labour.

He had tried to get his younger brother to take some of the load, but the little swine was not too keen. He had tried some of his father's treatment on him. But it did not work very well.

His grandmother, who had begun to spend more time huddled by the fire, died. They buried her on the farm beside where her husband lay. She had never made a fuss of him, nor he of her, and the only thing he felt was that it made a bit more room for everybody. She was past working and nobody seemed to miss her.

He had not noticed that some of the sheep were rubbing themselves, until he saw the tufts of wool on the bushes. He thought that they were maybe too warm, as the good weather had not let up for days. When he brought them in at night they still continued to rub. John had been working early in the morning and coming back late in the afternoon and had not bothered to look at them.

"How be the sheep, boy?" he asked one night.

"Fine," said Jacob. "They be feeling the heat methinks."

"How?"

"They keep rubbing."

"They what?" snapped his father.

"Well it hath been overwarm these last days," explained Jacob.

"And in the pen at night?"

"The same."

John went very still, as swearing men do when they get a real shock.

"Come," he said, and Jacob went with him. John only needed one glance over the backs of the penned sheep. "The buggers have got the bloody scab," he growled. Jacob stood back at the vicious tone in his father's voice. "That bastard bailiff and his bloody bargains."

"What be it?" asked Jacob.

"Thou wilt see in the morning," was all his father would tell him.

Jacob did see in the morning.

"Lil," said his father to his mother, "ye do the milking. Boy come wi' me."

In the pen most of the sheep were rubbing as if itchy, some had worn the wool right off in patches, showing red bleeding sores. One look was enough for John.

"Keep them penned till I get back. Busy thyself with some other work." And he walked away.

It was not until he had gone that Jacob noticed that his father had not had any breakfast. Jacob and his mother saw to the milking and feeding the stock.

"Take the oxen out and tether them to graze," said his mother.

"What is scab?" Jacob wanted to know.

"Thou wilt know soon enough when thy father gets back. Just tether the oxen and tidy the box up. Feed that calf."

Some time later John arrived, his broad shoulders sagging with a bucket of tar in each hand.

"What of it?" asked his mother.

"They have it themselves, up at the Manor. These cheap ewes. He should have regarded them better before he bought them. Anyway he be giving me three days wages off the price, and two buckets of tar besides. Let us have some vittals to eat afore we start."

The concessions from the bailiff seemed to have cooled him down.

Jacob found what it meant to get started, and also the work that they had to do before they finished. The fury of his father's anger had steadied to a slow burn, only the steely look in his eyes showed any difference from his usual taciturn nature. Jacob and his mother waited quietly. They would be told what to do in his father's good time.

"Tis needful to make another pen," he said at last.

They found some stakes to make one next to the one holding the sheep. John laid a cloth in one corner and produced some cord and shears. He went into the pen and grabbed a ewe and swung it off its legs and onto the cloth, made a quick half hitch round its legs and proceeded to cut the wool off. The wool was not quite ready to rise as it does in the annual moult and made the clipping harder, but he made a fair job of it.

"Fetch the tar," he ordered Jacob, when he had finished the first one. "Now then, paint it there and there upon the sore. Not on thyself ye stupid clot."

That was the only orders that Jacob had that day. He was supposed to know what to do after that. His mother knew what her duties were, taking care of the wool. His father kept on with a non-stop drive but it took a lot longer than a normal shearing would take, the little ticks and sores making the sheep wriggle and jump when John passed the shears over the bad places. This meant more whetting of the shears to take the strain off his forearms from the extra pressure.

It was no good getting rough with them and John guided his temper into saving his energy. He was used to slipping the shears under the fleece and rolling it off in an unbroken pelt in an effortless rhythm. Once they had started they had to finish, but his mother fetched out some ale and bread to keep them going. Jacob did his best but his opinion of the nice quiet sheep that he had been tending was changed that day. Aching and weary, plastered with sheep muck and tar he vowed that he would never work with sheep again.

His father was in a better mood by the time they had finished and filled the fresh pen with the shorn ewes. When he calculated what they had cost him in money he nodded to his wife with the nearest to a quiet smile that they had seen. He even deigned to show Jacob 'the little buggers' that had been biting the sheep and caused all the bother.

"Let us to the ale mistress," he called.

It was the first time that Jacob tasted the full first ale. He lay on his pallet that night and nearly forgot the troubles of the day.

His father was even better pleased when he found that he had managed to sell his wool before the price had dropped by two shillings a tod shortly after.

Jacob continued with his milking and sheep tending as usual. Now that he knew what to look for, the occasional dab with his tar brush kept 'the little buggers' at bay. When it came to blow-fly time his father made sure that he knew what to look for and, with the wool on the sheep being shorter than usual for the time of year, he was spared the frustration of dagging the soiled wool off the ewes tails and scraping off the maggots caused by the flies. He spent his tending time recovering the bunches of wool which the sheep had rubbed off, and added that to the shearing clip.

When it came to the real shearing on the Manor he was counted big enough to go and help his father at his obligatory stint. It was the first time that he had the chance to work with a crowd of men. His father's attitude had taught him to fend for himself and the men soon saw that he could be relied on, and accepted him as skilled men do.

John had sold their sheep back to the demesne flock and bargained with the bailiff to claim his share of grazing a few sheep in the common flock. That was the last of the sheep as far as Jacob was concerned, except for one which they killed for themselves and salted.

At the Shearing Ale feast Jacob was counted as a boy and had to do with the watered down brew which he usually drank.

Most weeks his mother had been making the ale in a shed where she had the oven for bread making. John's father had made a deal with the Manor to be allowed to make his own bread and John carried on the concession. Jacob's mother brewed the ale first and made the batch of bread on another day.

There was a man at Tibberton who had a malting floor but the bread meal had to be ground at the manor mill. This was another complaint of his father as he blamed the miller for returning short measure. It pleased his heart that his wife had a small stone quern which she used for grinding roasted barley to give the ales some colour and to grind some extra rye for the bread. His father had taken the precaution to warn Jacob that 'such doings were not a matter for gossip'. Jacob began to think that there were many things that were not a matter of gossip, and stored it up for the future.

At first he had watched his mother brewing and then, as he grew stronger, found himself with the task of fetching the water to fill the large iron pot, and the wood and bracken for the fire which she lit underneath it. She was a bit more forthcoming than his father and, although she claimed that it was a woman's job, she showed him how it was done.

"First make a good boil with the water and then put in the malt and, when it be ready, the balm. Then when it be ready, skim off the balm to keep for another time and to use for to make the bread to rise. Then, when the brew be ready, with this ladle take out the ale into these earthenware pots."

"How knowest thou when it be ready?"

"My mother did tell me. It be the work of the women."

Jacob wondered how anyone managed to learn the difference between men's work as assumed by his father and woman's work as hinted by his mother. But he kept his eyes and ears wide open and, if it made him as secretive as them, at least it was all stored up for the future.

"The first ladling be for the men," she said. "The second for the women and children."

The husks that were left were good to chew, but were used to tempt the sow in at night time from her foraging in the spinneys.

"When will I be a man?" asked Jacob, thinking of the first ale.

"Not long now," she said, "not long now." Partly with pride, partly with sadness. After all, he was her firstborn and she knew that he would not be the heir.

As far as Jacob could remember, the sow pig that they had, always had little ones running with her in the spring and summer. She would spend the days scuffling the earth and finding fallen acorns and nuts in the spinney and foraging in the fields after the harvest had been gathered. It had fallen to Jacob to tempt her home in the evening by calling and feeding her the brewing mash.

When the little ones grew up they were sold, or killed and salted at killing time, before the winter set in. Then, in the spring, some new ones would appear from somewhere. One year John kept one of the young ones alive at killing time.

"Twill make company for the old one in the winter," he told Jacob. "Feed her well."

She was a well grown gilt by late winter when John told him, "In the morning keep the sows penned. I will have need of thee anon."

In the morning, after the daily chores were finished and they had their breakfast his father said, "fetch a paddle. We take the young sow to the manor yard."

"What for?"

"The paddle is to guide her. I will have one on the other side."

That was not what Jacob meant but it was all that he was going to be told. He did find out what the paddle was for. The gilt seemed to have a mind of her own and was not going to be separated from the place where she had been born and had grown up in. It was a warm job on a cold day. Fortunately the ground was frost dry, better than trailing through mud. They were near the yard before the animal took it into its head to go straight for the building.

"Ho John," shouted the bailiff who had seen them coming. "Art here then? He's well ready for her."

Jacob saw the head of another pig appear over a door in a pen. It seemed to be trying to climb out, the froth slavering from its mouth.

"Aye, let him out," said John. "She be well ready for him."

The bailiff withdrew a bar off the door and the captive pig rushed out and went straight for Jacob's pet and, getting his snout under her belly, lifted her off the ground. They circled each other as she tried to nuzzle him and he tried to get his head on her hams.

Jacob saw the redness shining out of the boar's belly as he mounted and pushed into her, while she stood willingly to his service. The boar rested from his labours, his head cocked to one side as if listening for something. Then he set about her again. Jacob looked at his father who was talking to the bailiff and taking no notice.

After a while the boar slid off the gilts back and John and the bailiff acted quickly to separate the two pigs and drive the boar back into his pen.

"Now, boy. Back home. A good job done this day."

"What was all that about?" asked Jacob.

"Eh? Oh, five or six young pigs come Spring, please God. Twill be enough for her to rear. When ye see the red shining like that she'll be ready again."

Jacob saw the red glow under her tail and looked away. Another piece of education to be used in a future time.

"She will remember the road to go the next time, like the old one, and will take no driving," laughed his father.

CHAPTER THREE

One day, his father, who had taken note of Jacob's success at the communal shearing, "twould he better for thee to work some time on the demesne land, instead of filling in thy time doing nothing at home." He did not say anything about Jacob getting wages.

Sometimes Jacob found himself setting off, after the morning milking, to join the other youngsters in the corn weeding, bird scaring and hay raking, as well as getting into mischief. In the evening he was back to milk his cow and feed his calf.

When he heard the other youngsters talking of a school in Tibberton he asked his mother about it.

"Tis right," she said. "I did go to it. But that was the wish of my father. Twas run by the pastor. Thy father went not to any school. I surmise that you will do well without it."

He found that there were many things that he had thought were usual, that the other youngsters did not have to do. At first it unsettled him, but his father still had an overbearing effect on him and he did not dare to ask about it. He asked his mother one day, to be greeted with a surprised silence for a moment or two.

"Aye, that may well be," she answered as she thought about it. "They be peasants," she said. "But we be freemen and have rent land of our own."

"What meanest thou?"

"It means that which we make, we keep...if God doth give us an increase...and we can go where it pleaseth us without let or hindrance from the manor. Thy uncles at Tibberton are free but have no land. They be Gebures with their house and tools from the Manor, but the chattels go back to the Manor when they die." Jacob thought about it. "On this holding there be not enough to keep us all," she told him, "and thy father hath to work two days a week on the Manor for no money as our rent, and other days at harvest times." It was a lot for a boy to consider. "Thou dost work well," she told him. "Some day, if ye do your work to what thou dost know, ye will be a skilled man."

"And take the virgate of my father when he is old?" he asked, with a sly touch of sarcasm.

He was surprised at the steady, almost sorrowful look in his mother's eyes.

"That will be bye and bye," she said and left it at that.

When Jacob was eight years old, his father had in mind to use his other children on his own holding and hire Jacob to the manor on full time day wages according to his age. This brought a whole new world and a new set of problems to the lad who had been used to working by himself.

He had not grown to a great stature, but he was hard built and his father had always required him to work to his strength. It had pleased Jacob to try and aim for the best that he could do, and his father's strength was always a spur to him. But now he found that the aim of his young workmates was to get away with as much as they could manage. The bailiff also, taken in by his size, allowed him jobs in accordance with the others of his build.

What would he do? His mind had developed a cunning in the seven years' hard work. Now, he decided, that as he was working for the bailiff, and not under his father's driving force, he would do what he had to do...just enough to satisfy the expectations of the bailiff.

He found that the expectations of the other workers, both young and old, was another problem. The older workers, who knew his father' ability, and some of them his father's father before him, treated him with a quiet acceptance.

Not so the younger crew. Jacob had assumed that if he was in a gang, then it was enough to match their efforts. He had never experienced a pecking order although he did notice that one of them seemed to be the leader. It did not bother him as he had to leave them at night to do his milking and was not involved with them away from work. The leader, as usual, was the oldest, and the biggest. He was a tall-for-his-age gangly sort of lad with tousled hair and a weak mouth. He was annoyed that Jacob didn't allow him the right to boss him, as he did the rest the gang.

One day the youngsters were weeding corn on their own, behind a spinney, and out of sight of any supervision. At the end of the field they decided on some relaxation and started playing about in the wood. Jacob, used to working on his own, and without the necessity of having his father's domineering presence, was all for carrying on with the work.

"Look thee here," said the tall lad. "If we do take it easy when out of sight, then ye do as we do."

"I do as it damn well pleaseth me," said Jacob.

"Thou wilt do as I do tell thee," said the lad, coming up to him and pointing his finger. "Make thou no mistake."

Unfortunately his pointing finger poked into Jacob's chest. A flush of adrenaline made Jacob move by instinct. He felt an excruciating pain in his hand which spread up to his elbow and into his shoulder. At his feet the lad was lying prostrate.

There was a sudden silence until one of the girls shrieked, "Thou hast killed him. Tam is dead."

Jacob felt himself go cold, as he thought of the terrible consequences, until Tam stirred and rolled on to his back, stroking his jaw. Jacob rubbed his bruised knuckles and looked at Tam, as he felt the anger drain from him.

"Thou dost look after y'r own," he said. "I take none of thy orders. If ye say ought to anyone about this, there will be more for ye."

Some of the girls were fussing round Tam when the oldest one came to have a look at Jacob's hand.

"You don't know your own strength," she laughed.

She was buxom, Saxon blond and blue eyed, with a round peasant's face. She was not much taller than him but her bulk seemed to overpower him. He was not equipped to deal with such a situation. He was now on an eye level with his mother, and his sisters seemed puny things.

The full red lips parted to show a flash of strong white teeth as she bent to kiss his bruised knuckles. He stood petrified as the warm wetness soothed the pain. She slyly turned his hand and ran her tongue down his fingers and over the palm, round the swelling of his thumb.

She laughed up into his face, staring hard like a weasel, as she felt him jump at her touch.

"The next time that you have a chance to frolic in the wood," she said, "I could show you a thing or two that could be better than pulling thistles."

He looked at her, the gentle touch of her fingers easing the pain in his shoulder. He felt strangely excited, the fighting blood lust simmering down. Her hands had a different effect from Tam's prodding finger and he wondered what she meant. In her wordly wisdom she turned away with a smile. And left him to wonder.

Whether it was his acceptance by the girl, or his feat in downing Tam with one blow, he was taken as one of the gang from that day on. Whether Tam kept his silence or not, the older men must have heard about it and, although not saying anything, treated Jacob with a muted respect.

Not so the bailiff. He must have heard of the fracas, as

was his duty to know all that happened on the estate. Not that he mentioned it, but Jacob began to find himself doing tasks away from the other youngsters which needed his full strength. The result was that he would trail home weary at the end of the day and roll into the straw dead tired.

Of course, he still had the milking chores to do. One night he was longer than usual bringing in the milk, and his mother found him fast asleep with the bucket between his knees and his head against the warm flank of the cow.

"What ails thee, Jacob?" she asked, as she quietly wakened him.

"Nothing," he said.

"There be something." She sounded concerned.

"Well," he said at last. "It seems I be getting the hard tasks now."

"The bailiff?"

"Aye."

She pondered a moment. "He be a wicked man that Bailiff...and a coward. He be getting his own back at thee, for jealousy of thy father who is a better man than he is at his tasks. Thou wilt be the better for it...if thou canst bear it for a while."

It seemed to satisfy Jacob who hunched his shoulders in resignation.

"Take no notice or he will be worse. He can be."

She knew that it was not John who the bailiff was getting at...it was her. She knew the power he had over the peasants' lives, and how he enjoyed using it. He had taken her many times, refusing her denials, and used her without thought for her safety. He had never even paid for the potions from the witch on the banks of the Meese.

Now she was frightened about John's reaction if he found out. Especially if he had to contain himself and lose his self respect.

Jacob began to find that the new companionship when he was working in company was more enjoyable than being on his own, and never grumbled that his father had made him work on the manor land. He would have liked to go back in the evenings to see the girl but his father found him enough work to keep him at home.

The fact that he never saw the money that he earned on the demesne land was a constant irritation in his mind but a quiet slyness had grown in him as he took notice of the other workers and gave only what he thought was his due. But, deep down, the frustration was there and the knowledge that money, and especially land, meant freedom.

'Some day,' he thought, 'I will have some money.'

He thought of his ox calf and the others that had followed, and what he had learned. 'The oxen is where the money will come from.' How, or when, he knew not.

Jacob had not been allowed to go to the Caynton Manor feasts when he was young, but his father would go off without the oxen and come back the worse for drink. When he had been contracted to the work on the demesne, the other youngsters had expected him to attend and, perforce, his father could find no objection so long as the milking was done in the morning and when he came home in the evening. The men would sit around and drink while the younger people were allowed to wander off into the woods.

It was a good time for Jacob, as he managed to slip away from the others with his newfound girl friend. He had found out that her name was Gill and that she lived on the Tibberton estate.

"Short for Gillyflower," she told him. "I came when the flowers brightened the days after the winter."

"What dost thy father do?" he asked her one day.

She went quiet and looked away. "I have no father."

"Tis needs that ye have a father and mother," he said in his naivety.

She laughed, a deep scathing shake of her shoulders, without mirth. "Aye, there was a man who put me inside my mother... and other brothers and sisters besides."

"What meanest thou? Did he die?"

She looked at him with almost compassion in her age old eyes. "We live on the Knight's Acre at Tibberton. Did you not hear of Hewlin of the Knight's Meadow who never returned from the Inn one night?" He shook his head. "He hied himself off somewhere and took Payne of the Willows to accompany him." He did not understand. "Everyone said that they went to Shrewsbury to hide themselves for a year and a day, to rid themselves of their serf bondage." He waited for more, having nothing to say. "Tis been long years and no word from him...and no work on the Knight's land to occupy me, so I must needs find work here."

He had been irritated by a father who tried to get the most out of him. But at least he did have a father.

"I remember now. My father said, when they talked about these men, that it was out of the frying pan into the fire...if they had the plague to contend with."

"Tis not a thought to dwell upon," she said, crossing herself. "You are but a boy, kept by your father from the ways of the world," she laughed.

He reared up at the implied insult. "I be well skilled to my age, and soon will be man grown."

"Nay, take it not to heart. You are well forward for your age, but there are many things besides being knee deep in mud and with your nose stuck up an oxen's arse all day, ploughing for others to take the gain from the sweat of your brow."

"What meanest thou?"

He looked at her, lying full length in the boudoir that

they had made among the ferns, and felt a tantalising promise of something that had not as yet, entered his expectations. She lay quiet as if in another world. For the first time he noticed the sheen of her uncovered hair and the whiteness and quality of her smock showing under her kilted skirts, as compared with that of his sisters and mother.

The lacings of her short sleeved kirtle were slackened and pushed aside by, what he had considered, good feeding compared with his mother's flat chest. She splayed her legs as she turned to him and he felt an unexpected thrill as she outlined her thighs in the thin woven material.

"You don't know the Gentry," she said in a kindly voice. He knew not the answer to that. "The Caynton lords are only small Gentry, they hold their land under the Lords of Bolas, by right of the King's Foresters...You don't know the Edgmond Lord?"

"Only at Easter, when we go to Church to drink the wine."

She laughed, deep in her throat. "As the parson says from the Bible, they toil not, neither do they spin....."

Suddenly she came up on her elbow, looking him straight in the eye. "But they do know the way to enjoy their life."

"How knowest thee all these things?"

She brightened up. "You should see the knight in his array when he goes to the tournaments...and when he returns...."

She left it at that, smiling at the memories.

"What?"

She looked at him with laughter in her eyes. "If he has won, as he mostly does, he sends for my mother to join his pleasure...and we certainly live well for a time."

"But...but...?"

"The knight has shown me the way of the

tournaments..and the way of talking like the Gentry..and now that I am well fashioned," she hugged her breasts, "the jollifications that they have...after......He calls me Jouette." He still had no knowledge of the matter. "Come, I will show you."

And she did. He felt the lissom strength of her arms as they wrapped round him as she pulled him towards her.

He was kept busy between work on their own holding and the demesne work, but the memory of the afternoon in the wood was a continual problem. When his tasks meant that he was near Gill, she was friendly but in a distant way, without disregarding him.

"Let the peasants think as they will," she told him as an aside, while she looked at the other workers. "But give them no reason to guess what they should not know."

It was not to his liking, but he had enough practice of dissembling with his family to realise that there would be trouble if suspicion became knowledge.

However, one night his ruthless streak overcame his caution. He had been out checking his coney snares and found that he had caught two rabbits. As he had made a corner for himself in the byre where he could sleep, he was able to come and go in the evening without the rest of the family knowing where he went. So, in the morning, he presented one of his catch to his mother and hid the other one.

He had heard that the knight had come home for one of his visits and Gill had not come to work. So, the next night he set off on the quickest route to Tibberton and was fortunate to find the knight's house on the near side of the village. He waited a piece, wondering what to do, and was in luck again to see Gill come out of a house and go down the path to the Privy. He was surprised at the antagonism she showed when he made himself known to her.

"You should never come to this manor," she told him. "If you do come, at any time for the Knight's homecoming, then I will not know you from the others."

"The knight? doth he absent himself many times?"

"There are many tournaments in many parts of the country and he takes his warhorse and two ponies with his esquire. He is gone for long sometimes...but if he gains much booty and is near at hand he sends word that he will arrive at such and such a time....and we prepare to be ready to make merry."

She lay back against the wall and smiled and he felt shut out of her thoughts; that it was a thing that he was not a part of.

"Sometimes," she said with a sudden change of mood, "he is sore hurt...but he is too skilled to suffer much. When he is in his cups he boasts of his deeds, but methinks sometimes he makes more of them than is possible."

"And the esquire?"

"I am not for him...and he knows it. There are plenty others for his amusement... Now. You have spent enough time in talking. There will be plenty times at the demesne feasts...and then you will be welcome."

In the morning he presented the other rabbit to his mother as a reason for the supposed night's poaching. But when he came to eat his share it tasted like sawdust.

As he had said, they always went to Edgmond at Easter for the yearly communion as it was the main Church in the area. They had been at other times for christenings and sometimes he had gone with his father on a Sunday. 'To pay their respects to the Church,' his father had told him. Really it was only when his father had some business which needed attention that caused him 'to waste the time away from his home.' He would spend the time after the church service in the Inn, with the order to 'be ready when I do call thee.'

It did not give Jacob much of a chance to learn anything about the place, or the people, as he felt an outsider and not very well dressed, and he was glad when the time came to get back to his usual haunts. Even then he was irritated by the comparison of the shortcomings of his life.

As the days went by, if he was working on his own, he had time to think about his plight. All his life he had been kicking against something, without a plan of action. Tied to his father; tied to a farm which would go to his younger brother; working for somebody else's good. Gill's mention of the Edgmond Manor aroused his speculation and he made the excuse, which his father could not gainsay, that he ought to go to the Church once in a while. The time spent on Sunday afternoons after Church was limited by having to get home to see to the oxen.

He asked Gill one day, "There be a tall dark man at Edgmond who the people touch their caps to. Is he the Gentry?'.

"Nay. He is Alleyn, the Clerk to the Estate. He keeps the records for when the Auditors come once a year at Michaelmas. The gossip is that he acts like the Gentry....and his sons."

"In what way?"

"They don't do any land work...except the young one."

"With the red hair?"

"Aye. They will not speak to you. You are but a serf."

"My mother says that we be freemen and can do what we will."

She looked at him as if to say something, then on an impulse she grabbed him in a moment of compassion.

"So long as it is not against the custom of the manor,"

she laughed and, in the ensuing pleasantries, saved herself the task of explaining that even freemen are bound by the need for money and a place to live.

When he was working on the demesne land at Caynton his mind was sharpened to notice the workers; the youngsters of his own age; the apathy of their ambitions; the stoic indifference of the adults. But the mention of the brothers at Edgmond had awakened the memories of times that he would have liked to stay for an hour or two after the church service.

On the Sundays he began to take more notice of the Edgmond village and the activities of the villagers, the men at the butts or wrestling, the children playing around while the women sat and gossiped. There were many more houses than he was used to, some of them scattered about, built in a piece of land. He had a look at the gardens and the general prosperity of the estate. It was the sort of life he wanted. But an impossible dream.

CHAPTER FOUR

Jacob had gone, twice, to see the knight return from his forays and joined in the feast with the others but, as she had warned him, Gill acted as if she did not know him any better than the others.

On his second visit he was standing with a group of lads of his own age when Gill came to them. She was dressed in a better style of clothes than he was used to seeing, and held herself with an air of superiority.

She was wearing a gown with the bodice showing the swell of her breasts and tight fitting at the waist. The skirt was full and swept the ground. The usual skimpy veil was replaced by one which was much folded and pinned higher on her head and had a darker cloth, matching her gown, falling over her shoulders.

"You must comport yourselves with respect, this day," she told the boys in her Gentry voice. "The last time that you were here, Tom Bower's son, you did gorge yourself to bursting. See to it that you be more circumspect."

Just then the knight joined them. "A goodly band of rascals," he laughed. He had a twinkle in his dark eyes, his short cropped beard, black in his brown face. "Any good bowmen among you?"

They stood abashed in his presence, unused to such familiarity from the Gentry. They scuffled their feet in embarrassment, looking at each other with downcast eyes.

Jacob was surprised at his own reaction. He could never remember what the knight wore. All he could concentrate on was the face, and the eyes which seemed amused. But he felt that behind them was a steely intent, and he could imagine the relaxed frame springing into violent action in an affray.

He saw the knight's eyes harden as his glance met Jacob's stare. Slowly the assessment took in his face, and manner, and clothes. "A wolf among the flock?" he queried.

Gill, noticing the look and hearing the suggestion in the words, quickly broke in. "My Lord, he is Jacob, the son of John of Caynton Moor. I have seen him on the Caynton demesne land, on the occasion of my visits there."

"I know your father." His tone was neither praising or condemning. "A freeman... A strong man but not one to waste his time in revelry." Whether that opinion was a good thing or not, Jacob never found out.

"A strong youth...and a freemen." Sir Richard gave the merest inclination of a bow, which on other occasions might have given an affront, and turned to Gill. "I have need of you to serve some guests," he said and walked away, his broad shoulders swinging with arrogant ease. The tinkling music of his spurs heralded his going.

Gill walked behind him, straight backed and proud, as a handmaiden should.

Although Jacob still had the fierce knowledge of his free status, he had to behave himself as one of the lower orders when he was on the Tibberton estate. It did not suit his pride and he did not go a third time.

He did not realise that, when he was learning the pleasures of the body, Gill had tried to teach him the possibilities of a life above the serf labour that he had been born into. But he had begun to think that there were many things about the Edgmond estate and its organisation that he wanted to find out.

It might have been better if he had known the difficulties that beset his path. But that might have destroyed his dream, or stirred his fighting spirit and made him hard and selfcentred like his father.

He found that, when he spent his Sunday afternoons in the Edgmond village, he was faced with another problem. Regarded as a stranger, and not a very well dressed one at that. Gill had told him that, throughout the Country, rank was indicated by how one was dressed, and a newcomer judged by it. There were, of course among the common people, those who had aspirations above their station. Their advertisement was limited to the neatness and cleaness of their clothes, rather than the quality of the material. He could not help but compare them with his father and mother and their style of dress. Not for the better. Nor indeed his own.

Both by his age and his clothes Jacob found himself limited to the company of the young labourers and had to make his mark in the wrestling and other rough pursuits. Archery was compulsory among the men, as a training for any warlike occasion, but as he had no bow, he was limited to watching and, in any case, would not be counted in the local trained band which was organised as the means, if need be, for protection on the Edgmond estate.

He had noticed two of the better dressed men who were not a great deal older than himself, tall, dark haired, and with an air of authority which the other men assented to. He soon found out that they were The Clerk's sons and eyed them from afar.

One of his companions at wrestling had red hair, and wore a smock to assist him in joining the rough games. They were both of a size and strength and soon a competitive friendship grew between them.

"What do you here, and what is your name?" Jacob was asked one day, after a strenuous bout which left neither of them with the ascendency.

"Jacob from the Caynton Manor."

"Oh, aye?"

"What dost thou mean, oh aye?"

The red head laughed with mischief in his eyes. "I am Roger, son of Alleyn le Clerk. In a village there is much gossip. "Jacob bridled at that but his companion soothed him down. "Take it not to heart. I am the subject of much gossip as well. It brightens the peasant's lives to have someone to talk about...that is not of their station."

"But thou art the son of the Clerk, and yet thou dost comport thyself with the common youngsters."

Roger looked at him with a wary look in his eyes. At last he said "It is common talk that you are a freemen born, and yet you work, and live, like a serf... as equal. What say you to that?"

Jacob looked away, thinking of the talks that he had with Gill.

Roger waited and then, "My father and brothers and I are all bound to the Manor. But we live well and have a parcel of land to cultivate, have other perquisites, and are better educated....but we know that we are not free to do as we wish."

They faced each other, silently questioning each other. Roger looked across to where the archers were finishing their afternoon practice, he nodded in their direction.

"My brothers take after my father, they would be the Gentry if they could. I take after my mother and work the land which we are allowed. I act to suit the company that I work with, but they must try to show their breeding." It was something to puzzle Jacob, when Roger laughed at the thought. "There is much that goes on in the Nation which is the concern of my father in his position. Many changes since the great plague killed many workers...and those that are left seek their freedom to go where they list and demand day wages of a certain standard."

"Tis not the right of any man to own the life of

another...and his woman and his chattels."

Roger looked surprised, and taken aback at such an outburst.

"There are many of good standing who are tied to their manors by way of rendering different services," he said, "and there are still the workers who are subservient to the wish of the manor lords....It has always been so...and now there are those like you..." He let the question hang in the air.

Jacob was nonplussed. He had thought his unformed thoughts for years but had never met anyone who had brought them to the stage of expression.

"I have never been to school," he said," I know not the way of saying things...I only know what I feel...and the way of working to my knowledge."

They sat quiet for a while as they watched the men drift of in all directions, some towards the Inn. Roger's two brothers, with their bows over their shoulders were walking, quietly engaged in conversation.

Jacob noticed the arrogant swing of their thighs in the well woven quality hose, the skirts of their doublets shortened to mid-buttocks. The gaping front of the collarless doublets, loose laced, showed the fine linen of their shirts. A small rounded bonnet allowed their hair to fall to shoulder length.

"They don't know the way to enjoy themselves," said Roger, as they went past. "Besides they need someone like you and me to work the land and produce the food and wherewithall to keep them in the style to which they are accustomed."

"Thou hast a way of saying things."

"Fret not at my speech. I must needs speak to my father's instruction.....with the French at times." He broke into the common accent. "But I be an Englishman such as thou art, and act not above the station of those I toil with. Tis time I did go to the home of my father for my vittals."

So began a tentative friendship which grew as the months went by and fused into a comradeship which disregarded the age old customs which might have separated them.

The months were busy ones on the Caynton Manor. First there was hay harvest and then the corn harvest, enough to keep Jacob's body fully occupied following the reapers and turning the hay and pitching to the carts when they led it to the stackyard. At corn harvest he was allowed to bunch the corn behind the men scything and passed them to the women who drew the straw into long strands and, with a quick twist-knot bound the sheaves, ready for the stooks. The weather was cold with periods of rain, and even in the dry times the drying was tardy. His visits to Edgmond were few and not so boisterous, and they had led to another problem to excercise his mind. After some thought, he approached his father about the money that he was earning.

"I be due some of that in my purse," he told him.

"Thou hast had thy upbringing, and dost needfully pay for thy keep. Besides thou dost eat enough for two," was his father's opinion.

"I do enough work for two," Jacob took a gamble. "Thou knowest how I stand against the skivers with their shoddy work."

John was tough and more than a trifle greedy, but nevertheless he had a pride in his own work and made sure that he gained a proper price for it. He pushed his bonnet back to ruffle his hair as if in deep contemplation.

"And the money," he asked, "be it of a necessity?"

"The money that I should have would be mine, to do with as I please," said Jacob in a daring mood, which strangely enough roused a spark of appreciation in his father's opinion of him.

"Tis so," he said, "Tis so, but a word of advice maybe?"

Jacob, partly surprised at the offered consideration, partly softened by the unaccustomed sop to his upbringing, was put off his original aggression.

"When I visit Edgmond, there be times when I might visit the Inn for sustenance, which I may not do without money." He had a sudden resurgence of his intention, and suggested slyly, "it be not proper for a freeman with no money to mix with serfs who pay for their wants...and there are the dues for the church."

John knew that he had made sure of paying the dues which the Church demanded but he let that pass. More as a respect for the way in which his son had conducted the affair, he allowed himself to get the worst of the bargain, or nearly so.

"When thou dost do thy visiting...and waste my time, I will see that thou hast some of my hard earned savings to squander," he said.

Jacob had enough sense to realise his victory and did not press the matter further. But he did not bother to offer any thanks.

On his occasional visits Jacob was able to call on the Inn for some penny ale and sometimes some bread and cheese to fortify him. On one visit he was ribbed by some of the older men.

"Now that thou art a man, thou shouldst be able to take thy drink. In respect for thy manhood, take thee a pot of full ale instead of thy penny draught."

It took him some time to down the oblation, but he did manage to walk out of the inn without stumbling, and reach the outskirts of the village before the unaccustomed strong ale was retched out of him. Fortunately, for his future reputation, he was not seen by anyone as his stomach rejected the fullness.

Roger never accompanied him to the Inn on such excursions but one Sunday afternoon on a balmy day in St. Luke's Summer they were lying taking their ease when Roger said, "Can you, perhaps, stand a night without much sleep?"

Jacob thought for a minute or two, considering whether Roger, a member of the other camp, was sufficiently trustworthy to hold some knowledge which could be of trouble to him.

"I have seen the moon, on an odd night or two, which did not affect my work on the next day," he ventured.

Roger seemed to disregard the implication. "It's now the middle of October. You know what happens on the last night?"

"Nay. tis naught to me."

"Ah. Well. You don't live in a village, so you have missed most of the fun of special days. It's not your fault."

"I know naught of these things."

"Well. You must know that the second day of November is All Saint's Day. On the evening before, it is rumoured that the witches and warlocks and such like creatures used to go abroad to do their devilment. It has been usual for some of us young ones... and sometimes the old young ones...." He laughed at the memories.

"Do what?"

"Oh, build a fire and made the excuse to have a coven."

"What be a coven?"

"It's supposed to be a witches' Mass. And we would drink and dance...and such like goings on."

"You want me to come?"

"No, no. It's like this. I can make an excuse not to go...the family think that I should stop joining in these things but..."

Jacob waited.

"If you and I dressed up we could have some sport."

"How?"

"We could get some white sheets and be real ghosts. It would need two of us to really surprise them."

Jacob, who had spent a life time with only his work, and an existence, to worry about, felt the tingle of excitement at the unexpected venture. It was something new and risky, far above the dread of the penalties of being caught poaching.

"If we get a white sheet to cover our fronts," Roger went on. "And join them to a black one to cover our backs, then when we turn round they won't see us. Now we're here. Now we're not. It will be a morning moon, and the night should be dark enough. What do you say?"

Jacob laughed. "Tis a great ploy. It doth seem that I have lacked the chance to have some real fun." He suddenly thought of Gill's words. 'Thy nose stuck up an oxen's arse all day.'

It took some organising, getting the material, and keeping it all a secret, but they met late on the night on the outskirts of the village and helped each other to dress. Roger, who knew more about these things, had manufactured some horns from tree branches and they practised their turns and supposedly ghostly noises.

"Let's to the churchyard, among the yew trees, and surprise them coming from late Mass through the village green," suggested Roger. "One on each side of the path."

The unrehearsed stratagem did not work as well as they would have liked, but the confusion it caused was enough to satisfy them, as they withdrew to plan the next steps.

"I heard that they are having a fire in Bird Cage Spinney," said Roger. "Let us go there and see what is afoot."

They saw the fire and heard the commotion a long while before they reached it.

Jacob's blood was up by this time. When they had crept up unseen and conned the gathering he heard himself say, "let us approach from either side and see if they scatter. If so, we may grab one for the devil's delight."

They did so and, in the confusion, Jacob saw a figure fleeing into the trees. Taking off his horns, he made an effort, pushing through the low branches and found himself grappling with one of the young women. When she felt the earthly strength of the ghostly arms she pulled his mask off and recognised him in the dim light.

"You bugger," she laughed as she gave in with abandon.

The long walk home was like a dream. But he was there in time to milk his cow and anyhow, he reckoned, it was not part of his life among his own family. And how much longer would that last?

Life goes on and winter, with its hardships, passes and summer comes in again. And it was a good summer. The summer before had a disastrous harvest, but this year the corn was standing thick with a good ear, and looked like providing a heavy yield. There had been enough rain in the spring to give it a good start, followed by clear days with heavy morning dews which helped the crops. The weeds were also enjoying the growing weather.

"There be some thistles in the wheat that we can do without," said his father one day. "Ye better stay at home from the demesne for a day or two. Take a spud and dig deep... a good two inches to get them out."

"Weeding is the job of a boy," said Jacob.

His father took no notice. "Thistles such as these are the job for a man. And scare these bleeding birds while ye are at it. They will have all our produce" And he walked away.

'Sod you,' thought Jacob, but he went and took his

frustration out on the thistles and docks.

That was when he met Norma.

Although he reckoned that bird scaring was not a job for a nearly grown man of eleven years old, he allowed that thistles were a man's job. So he hacked the thistle roots out and left them to kill-dry in the blazing sun. For some reason his father had not sent his brothers to scare the birds which were having a field day in the newly shot ears.

He had managed to sling-shoot two pigeons, which would be duly cooked. But the sparrows, circling in a chattering cloud, kept playing havoc with his concentration. They would swoop in, ready to alight and all he could do was shout and set them off on another approach. When he settled to his weeding they were there again to call for his attention.

The heat and the flies and a general frustration of doing a menial job were simmering close to boiling inside him when he noticed this little waif, her long black hair hanging from her head covering, wandering along from somewhere. She looked a skinny thing with a white face and large dark eyes.

"What dost thou here?" he asked her.

"I have ailed of the croup and am getting better," she said as if that was enough reason.

He had not noticed her before and wondered who she was and where she came from. The proper manner of her speech intrigued him, and the neatness of her smock and the little jacket round her shouders.

"Does thy mother know?"

"My mother is busy with work and pleased to see me in the fresh air."

She seemed bright and confident but it did seem strange that one so young should be abroad on her own.

"Who are ye?" he demanded.

"I am Norma, daughter of Alleyn le Clerk."

"Oh from Edgmond? Tis is a far step for one so young. I have heard of ye. Thy mother is Agnes o' the Pixley, and thy brother is Roger... My friend." he added.

"I have heard of you too."

She seemed sure of herself. It was getting out of hand for old young Jacob.

"What?" he asked.

"That you are a naughty boy," was the pert answer.

"Nay. Who sayest so?"

"My brothers say that you fight and poach and can drink first ale. Your father is John of the Caynton Moor...."

"Aye, 'tis so....a freeman" he answered scathingly, as children do.

"My Great-grandfather came here with my Lord Roger." She lifted her head and looked him straight in the eye.

He looked back at her. Then he noticed something in the dark brown eyes and the tilt of her head which answered the stubborn streak inside himself. There was a carriage in the shoulders which was different from his sisters, or any of the other Saxon girls.

"Can ye scare crows?" he queried, trying to recover the ascendency.

"I would have been, if I had not been unwell... If I stay, will you show me?"

"Maybe," he grudged.

She stood by and watched him shout, and sling the stones at the black thieves.

"Can I try?"

"Thou art too small for a sling. Ye can shout...if ye can."

He laughed at her squeaky yells but, for some reason in spite of his toughness, he curbed his sarcasm. It became a game between them, a thing that he found amusing. Perhaps the fact that they were on their own, away from observing eyes, led him to relax and enjoy her company.

"Tis time that ye returned to thy mother," he said at last. "She will be anxious for thy welfare."

"There is no one on the manor who would vex me," she said.

"I suppose not, but thou must go."

He watched her stride off on the path that he took to the village each Sunday. In her walk, her head held high, he had an unexpected vision of Gill following the knight.

He did not realise that the meeting was of any consequence. She was only a kid, the girls on his manor were all older than her and of more use for playing around with. And, as she inferred from her remarks, she was the daughter of The Clerk, and not one to befriend a lowly worker.

Besides he had Gill, a woman nearly grown. But the thought of the girl's brothers made him, for the first time, take the Edgmond Manor seriously into his calculations.

CHAPTER FIVE

The next year his father and mother had plenty on their mind, as there was a great drought from the end of March till the end of July with the grass being scarce and the yield from the corn looking to be on the light side. Jacob's mother, with another boy and two girls to take care of, was hard pressed to make the food go round.

"Tis the burden of being free that we must fend for ourselves," she told Jacob.

"Tis said that there be some famine in other parts of the country," said his father. "Tis of necessity that we make do as best we can. Tis a pity that most of the return from our holding is in corn."

"The poor yield will make it hard for me to keep the growing family in sustenance," his mother said. "The children must scour the spinneys for berries and nuts."

Although the swine ate them readily, the nuts were too sour for human food. There was no waste from the table for the stock, as the garden was stripped of all the greenery that the family could eat.

At killing time, before winter set in, John was in two minds whether to sell his usual surplus of stock, or salt them down and eat them. Especially when he found that the extra money could not buy food that was not there. It did not make his temper any better and he seemed to expect more work from Jacob for less food. He had the growing feeling that there must be a better way for him to live. But how?

After his meeting with Norma in the fields, Jacob had managed to meet her on a few occasions. Although it was not seemly that a rough lad like him should be conversing with the daughter of the Clerk, at times Norma found a way of being accidently near him. One Sunday they were passing the time of day when he saw a bent, old lady, on her own, going home from Church to a cottage that he had noticed on the outskirts of the Edgmond village. The garden was smothered in weeds and there was a general look of neglect about the place.

"Who is she?" asked Jacob.

"That's widow Turner," she said.

"Widow?"

"Yes, her husband died some years ago and her family have all left home. She lives on her own now. The Steward allows her to live in her cot, although there is no one there who works on the estate. Her man was a good carpenter and she was a good nursemaid to the Steward's children. The Steward honours their memory."

"Then 'twould be right if she had a worker living with her?" suggested Jacob.

"What have you in mind?"

"Tis of no use me living at home for no wages," he said.

"What? leave home and live here?"

"Why not?"

She gave it some thought. "You must see the Steward first."

"Where is he?"

She hesitated for a moment. "Leave it until next Sunday. I will see my father. He will know what to do."

And so it was arranged.

Jacob said nothing at home. It was usual for young adults to leave home if there was not enough work for them on their own Manor. Jacob knew his worth to his father, and he was just turned twelve years old. Old enough, and experienced enough, to earn a decent wage, he thought, even if not quite the usual age to leave home.

It was a long week for Jacob but he had learned to keep his own council. He argued the matter out on his own, not even consulting Gill. By the time Sunday came round again he had made up his mind to leave home, either to Edgmond or perhaps elsewhere. His mother had said that he was a freeman, not tied to any Manor. And Newborough was close at hand for a man who was willing to work. During all the years of his suppression at home that thought had always been with him.

'One day,' he had thought, 'one day.'

Was this the day?

During the Church service Jacob stood looking at Master Alleyn's straight back in the first pew, next to his three sons and the little girl who had not been surprised at his temerity. If he had listened to the sermon about the man with the one talent he might have taken heart but all Jacob could think off were those things which had built up in his mind over the years, and the lack of opportunity to do anything about them until today.

After the service Norma came to him. "I have to conduct you to my father," she said.

"What will he say?"

"I know not his business," was the answer. "He does not discuss these thing with us women folk."

Norma took him to her father who looked very stern.

"You are young to leave home," he said, looking down his patrician nose.

Jacob who had steeled himself for a question was nonplussed for a minute, but he said, "I be twelve years old, "...a man grown when there is work to do."

Alleyn's eyebrows rose at the spirit in the boy. "Oh? Such as?"

"I can dig and hoe and spread corn," said Jacob.

Alleyn tried to put him down. "And mow and thresh and pitch to a load like a common servant of husbandry?"

"I can use a flail at times to rest my father...and tie behind him and stook the sheaves at corn reaping time. I prick the oxen at plough times."

"But you are too young to plough...."

"I know oxen," said Jacob, before Alleyn had a chance to comment further.

Alleyn, schooled in hiding his emotions, especially in front of his underlings. "How so? What is there to know."

That surprised Jacob.

"I have milked and reared calves since before I was three years old. I have listened to the ploughmen talking...I can nearly plough...on light land," he added.

Alleyn favoured a small French beard which he stroked when he needed to disarm the opposition. He took his time. "Does not your father need you? There is a shortage of labour now that the plague has killed many workers."

"Tis needful for me to make my own way. My youngest brother will inherit one day...and I am a freeman born to go where I list." He cursed into himself as he realised the implied slight.

Alleyn was quick to notice the check in Jacob's demeanour.

"I know you not," he said. "But my boys say that you are strong and...and wilful."

Jacob knew that was right...a thing not to be encouraged by his betters. He realised his mistake and tried to correct it.

"It may be so, Master. I have had a hard master who brooked no mistakes, or my doing less than what is right. Tis a thing that one learns."

"And you wish to live with Widow Turner?"

"She hath a garden which could yield better...if tended better."

"Will she have you?"

"I can not live there with no wages. If I could work for day wages I can recompense her."

"I have seen her," Alleyn surprised him again. "If she will have you, I will find you plenty to do. And reward you accordingly."

He did not tell Jacob that he had made up his own mind, in spite of the reservations of his two eldest boys, and the wholehearted support of his daughter. He knew Jacob's father, who was also a wilful man, but a renowned worker. That was what the estate needed, good workers. Nevertheless he had his misgivings about the boy.

"I thank thee, Master," said Jacob and went to see the widow.

Widow Turner seemed prepared to meet him. "Thou hast a name for drinking strong drink. There is none in this house. I am only a poor widow woman."

Jacob had been reading faces for years and had been dissembling for just as long.

"I be only a poor helpless orphan," he said. "My mother, God rest her soul, used to water the second ale to make it go round."

He saw the sudden flash of fire in her pale blue eyes.

"Tis right what they say," she laughed. "You have the making of a right rogue. I did have one here for thirty years before God took him. We will do well together."

"I grant ye that Mistress," he said. And so began a friendship which lasted until he married.

It did not suit his father when Jacob broke the news to him and his mother.

"I have brought thee up," he rampaged. "and now that we need thee, thou art ready to bugger off and leave us when thy brothers and sisters need thy help."

"I have given thee good service," retorted Jacob. "All the days of my life till now. With no wages or recompense except food. I will have no part in the inheritance, and there is no future here. Thou hast two more boys. Make the lazy sods work as thou didst do to me."

His mother sat with hands clasped tight wondering what the result would be. It came to her that she had taken Jacob for granted and had not realised how he had felt all these years. Nevertheless it was not a woman's place to say her mind and she kept still and waited.

It came to John that something like this had happened before in his own life but he was not going to admit it to the others.

"There will be one less mouth for me to feed," grumbled his father. "Take thy leave in the morning." And turned and left him.

Jacob had set himself up for an outburst from his father and was disappointed at the lack of the expected confrontation.

His mother was not very pleased but she had to agree with his father. Jacob had found out what his mother had promised when she had said years before, 'bye and bye'.

When he moved in with Mrs. Turner he found that he was entering another life. It was as if he was born again. The hard rough treatment of his father had bred a selfish and suspicious streak in him with regard to other people. He had liked his mother but, together with his father, he had taken her for granted with no place for sentiment between them. Now he had to learn another way of dealing with the greater variety of people who were becoming part of his life at all times of the day. And Widow Turner with her little ways.

He was surprised at the first meal when the good lady bade him take off his bonnet, a thing he had never seen his father do.

"Tis a mark of respect to the Good Lord for providing us with the food," she had told him.

Jacob, who had known that it was the hard work of his body which had done the providing, felt irritated but, as she was a woman, he went along with it to please her. She seemed to read his mind. "Tis God who doth give the increase," she told him and left it at that.

It also looked as if he was destined to follow in the footsteps of Will Turner, as she always referred to her former husband. Apart from finding that he was a 'Good man', she never gave him a clue as to his actual looks. But Will Turner did this in the garden and that at work, and made the furniture in the house. It was all said in passing but he listened and acted accordingly and they got on famously. The change in himself was gradual, and he did not recognise it. But it was there, all the same.

She fed him as well as she could. Truly the garden was above her strength to cultivate but he soon had it cleared and found the remnants of the vegetable beds her husband had made in times past.

"I can sow and weed," she told him. "Tis a help to have one to do the heavy work."

He wanted to help her and had an idea how to do it. The free time, which he had at night, was spent roaming round the estate getting to know the parts where he hadn't worked during the day. He found that the demesne farm was on the moorland above the dip of the land down to a broad shallow valley which was full of meres and marshes and pools full of fish. He knew what to do but was worried that his new mother might be averse to cooking something which was not allowed by the custom of the Manor.

The first time that he brought two fish home he offered them to her without a word. She looked at them, but all she said was, "five small loaves and two small fishes were used to feed a multitude. These will do us well on fast days."

"We will eat them to the glory of God," he said and they both laughed.

He slipped out at dusk one evening and made his way north, away from the village. There was plenty of tree cover and he had his route marked out to make his going unseen to all, especially the gamekeeper.

He had been that way two nights before and set three snares for conies in a big spinney about half a mile away. He had set them hidden among the trees, just in case there happened to be a dead one in a snare and he was not able to clear them the next day. As there had been heavy rain the night before he had to stay at home.

The first two snares were empty but he was lucky with the third one, and glad that a fox had not been there before him. He undid the wire and reset the snare, took the dead animal, slit it's stomach and flipped the paunch out. Pulling up his smock he hung the coney on a belt and, covering it with his smock, prepared for the homeward journey.

Suddenly a black garbed figure barred his way. The pale face glimmered in the darkness. Jacob knew who it was...the gamekeeper's son...and was surprised that he had not heard his coming. Remembering Tam, he weighed him up for a strike, but held his peace.

"I followed thee from the village," said the figure. "Thou didst make plenty noise with y'r going, Ye'll make more with the extra swinging between thy legs."

Atherton was about a couple of years older than Jacob and like him, a solitary boy, probably because of the calling of his father.

"Not a very successful night," he said.

"I want only one," said Jacob.

"Art sure? There be somebody on the estate who is not so full of care."

"How meanest thou?"

"There be a man from Newborough who doth buy the conies from my father, but do sell more than he doth buy from us."

"Not me," Jacob shook his head.

"They be plentiful, and a pest at times," said Atherton. "One for the widow now and again, my father would allow. But not to sell for money to spend in the brewhouse, like some." He seemed lost in thought. "I would take it kindly, if ye did happen to see such a one."

It went against Jacob's nature to do the work that the gamekeeper should do, but the thought of the occasional rabbit for the widow, without the risk of a penalty, made up his mind.

"If thou dost want it so."

"Let us return home and I will teach thee the manner of walking without waking the whole village." and he glided off into the darkness.

Atherton stopped. "Ye do well at catching fish," he said.

"Never had any," said Jacob.

"I have seen thee do it," Atherton didn't seem to be bothered.

"If," he said, "when tis needful for me to catch them for the Manor, thou dost give me thy help. One or two might find a way into thy satchel. I hate the bloody things."

And so a bargain was made which lasted into the next generation. Both were young and ready for excitement and the fish were caught on poaching forays, although they could as well have been caught in full daylight.

Jacob's first year in his new home was a difficult time for him as he tried to adjust to a new set of values. He wasn't sure whether to give in to his irritation with Mrs. Turner's little ways or try to be as masterful as his father had been.

"How are you getting on with Widow Turner?" Norma asked him one day.

"She doth fuss a lot," he answered.

She laughed. "She served some time in the manor house, looking after the master's children," she said. "I think that she tried to bring her family up as she had learned."

"I be no Gentry."

She looked at him in an odd way. "You know what my brothers say about you?"

"What?"

"A free man without land."

That shook him, as he well knew the feeling. "But they be tied to the manor."

"My father enjoys land by the custom of the manor. There is a talk that the day will come when men can buy their freedom."

"And the land?"

"It will be held by rent or bought free of all ties."

"How know you all this?" He was interested.

"I have no part in their deliberations, as is the custom of the women folks, but they let me listen without restraint."

"Some day," he said. "Some day."

Although she was young, she was well tutored in the ways of the world.

"Keep that in mind," she said.

CHAPTER SIX

It took Jacob some time to adjust to the method of control of the bigger estate. He did not have any contact with Alleyn after the first meeting and the bailiff seemed a figure in the background. Jacob had to take his day to day orders from the reeve.

He had never been able to get any direction from his father and his mother's answers were always limited by her life style. He was finding that some of the things that he had taken for granted, or that he thought he knew, had to be reassessed in the new circumstances. He found a ready ear in the widow who was always willing to listen and pass a comment when necessary.

"The Reeve is different from the one at Caynton," he said to her one day, with a question in his voice.

"Aye, that could be," she answered. "Tis a bigger Manor here...and a busier one."

"There be the young reeve and the old reeve..."

"Aye, and the old reeve's father was the reeve before that."

"There were two different ones at Caynton...to my knowledge."

"Well the Lords here were pleased with the Reeves, and the young ones learned from their fathers."

"Do the reeves then run in the family?"

"Not everywhere, and it was not so here at one time. On some manors the workmen appoint the Reeves...every year. But the old reeve satisfied his lordship. So they kept it in the family. So long as there is one to follow."

"They do a good job and the men seem content."

"Well," she warned him. "Guard thy steps. They brook no slacking. Remember that still waters run deep."

"I tried my hand at ploughing when I was driving for Will Liversage, on the Sandy Moor."

"Did ye so? I hope you left it as it shoud be."

He shrugged his shoulders. "Twas cross ploughing a summer fallow and easy going."

"Another year, if you please him, the Reeve will have you winter ploughing and the summer fallows also. All the year round...if ye are capable."

"Tother day the reeve asked me about an ailing neat cow."

"And?"

"I gave him the answer he desired." He laughed quietly at the remembrance. "He did look surprised."

"Will Turner used to say that most of the ploughmen know more about the ploughs than they do of the oxen."

"I want the ploughing."

"In a year maybe. Fret not. There is much to learn of other things. You did well at the shearing they tell me."

"Thou hast been gossiping again. I like not the sheep. Although, at the shearing, Thom the shepherd did look upon me with favour."

"Everyman to his bent. In a year you will be grown to the plough and then you'll have two oxen to tend."

"Twill be better than having to fetch your neat cow at busy times."

The reeve was a squat man with a quiet manner of organising. When he gave his orders he appeared to be asking, but they were really 'take it or leave it'. It was an ideal way of avoiding confrontations and it worked very well, especially in the changing labour difficulties. Jacob was well used to being told what to do and left to get on with it. The Reeve tested him out on a variety of tasks and soon had his measure.

"He does try," he told Alleyn once. "But I commend him not to his face, in case he doth get above himself."

Alleyn laughed. They both knew their power over the lives of the people on their estate.

"And what of the oxen which he said that he knew?"

"Aye. Mebbe so. But he could do with an inch or two of stature to handle a plough. But he doth know the oxen's strength and, when he goads for the ploughmen, will not gainsay a lazy one. He will mend by keeping, never fear."

Norma had finished her schooling under the Pastor and Alleyn had installed her in the manor house as a lady's maid. It was not altogether to her liking, or her plans. But for the time being it sufficed.

One morning, when she was allowed some time off from her duties, she was helping her mother to knead some flour.

"You said Alleyn and Pierre were for books and for management and they have gone to Cambridge. Roger is a tiller of the soil," said Norma.

"Aye. Tis true."

"And me?"

"You?"

"Yes."

Her mother thought awhile then, "Men think that this is a world of men...for men. Some men use women as if they own them. But it is a chance for women to help men to better themselves. Albeit in a quiet way. Your father will have a plan for you."

"Have you helped my father?"

"He would have been lost with a namby pamby woman. Albeit he thinks that he makes his own decisions. He has made his determination of your life, have no doubt."

"He has said naught to me."

"No. But he has ordered ways to what he thinks will be best for you...and himself, of course."

"What?"

"You will see. I am only guessing." As if to forestall any further questions she changed the subject. "Now," she said as she rolled down the sleeves of her kirtle and began to lace them, "this batch of bread to rise. Then the churning of the butter while the bread bakes."

Norma meant to bring up the matter of Jacob but thought that the time was not quite right.

Jacob was growing, there was no doubt about that. During his first winter in Edgmond he had been seeking heavy work to build his strength and the occasional poaching raids had kept them supplied with meat. At pig killing time the widow had been supplied with some fresh meat from her neighbours and they had been able to salt down the pig that they had fed in her sty.

He was still much of a loner and seldom joined in with the rest of the young men in their games or visits to the Inn. He was interested in Maykin the blacksmith, as he was the nearest, in build, to his own father.

Maykin was a black man. Black head hair; black whiskers; thick black hair on his arms and chest where his shirt bulged open; black face where he had wiped the sweat with his sooty hands. He was also a big man, as Jacob's father had appeared to him when he was young. Now that he was older, his father would have been on an eye level with him. But Maykin was way above that. He was also strong. Stronger than even his father was.

The first time that Jacob had seen Maykin at work was one day when he heard the music coming from the forge. All his life he had been used to the woodpeckers in the trees and the Brrrrrip Tap Tap as they burrowed for the insects. This was different, as the bell like jangle spaced the solid thumps of a hammer. He went to have a look.

Maykin had an iron rod, red hot, laid on the anvil and was rattling his hammer in a musical beat on the metal between strokes, sparks flying all over the place. Rat-te-ta, THUMP, ta-ra-ra, THUMP, THUMP, THUMP, ta-ra-te-ta. A twist of the rod and THUMP, THUMP, THUMP, te-ra-ra. He shifted his hold on the rod and thrust it back into the fire and pulled the bellows one-handed with seeming ease, making the fire roar upwards. He twisted the rod with his other hand to get an even heat.

He looked at Jacob. "Couldst do this work, boy?"

Jacob shook his head.

"Have a try." He laid the spitting rod back on the anvil and pointed to a smaller hammer. "Use that one. Now, when I nod my head...you hit it." He let out a roar of laughter, which seemed to come from his belly, at the silly joke. He was a jolly man, with the kindly ways of men who know their own strength. Although Jacob thought of him as an old man, he was only in his late twenties.

Jacob tried and missed, and tried again.

"Tis easy," said Maykin, striking with his own hammer. THUMP, THUMP, he let his hammer trail along the anvil as if it spoke of its own accord, ta-ra-ra-re-ra, as if anybody could do it. Then his face went still as he stopped the hammer. "...Tis easy when thou hast done it as long as I have....wouldst like to learn?"

Jacob got into the habit of visiting him when he found the time and learned something of the blacksmith's art. It was not a job that he wanted to do all the time, but it helped to strengthen his arms, and made a friend for years to come.

In the community, which was bigger than the one at Caynton,

the feast days in the village were for everybody, with sports and drinking and dancing. Norma was working in the Manor House but joined in the merrymaking with the others. One Lammas Day feast Jacob managed to dance with her and it seemed natural to sit with her for a minute. He felt uncomfortable that she had grown so neat and beautiful.

"Nay, stay a minute," she said as he rose to leave. "It will be allowed on such a night as this."

After a while she said, "I go to glean herbs in the wood some evenings."

He was not quite sure how that affected him.

"That be no task for the maid of a lady."

"I work in the kitchen now, and am learning the ways of cooking for the Gentry."

"But thou didst say that thy father wanted thee as a maid for the ladies."

"That is not for me, fussing round people who should be able to look after themselves. They still keep a man as the Cook, as has been the habit of the Gentry. He is one of the old school and knows many things about the French Gentry food. However he is particular, and hard to satisfy."

Jacob, who knew the feeling of being regulated, kept quiet.

"Tis a hazardous job in the woods in the evenings," she ventured, in order to direct him to the way that she had in mind.

"Twould not be right for me to be with thee," he pointed out.

"Mistress Bancroft, the Housekeeper, says that it would be in order. To guard me from danger." She did not say what danger.

He was fifteen and cruelly tempted by the Manor girls. But the Clerk's daughter?

"Every night?" he asked.

"No. Tuesday and Thursday...for the Ember days."

He laughed deep in his throat. "Tis a good ploy to get us in a holy mood." He rose. "I will be there when thou dost reach the wood."

He told no one about it except the widow, who was curious when he disappeared on regular outings, but came back without any poaching plunder.

"You do play with fire, young Jacob." But it was said in a kindly vein.

Jacob was about sixteen when, one Sunday evening he returned from the butts feeling aggrieved. They had been shooting at a longer length and the bow, which he had managed to acquire, did not have the strength for accuracy. He was disappointed, as he had seen the widow among the onlookers.

Silently she filled a basin with potage and placed it on the table for him. He took off his bonnet and moved the spoon through the vegetables and felt something solid. He fetched it out and put it in his mouth and looked at the old lady. Her eyes were expressionless.

"One of the kitchen maids," she said, "happened to drop a parcel as she went by."

"Who?"

"I saw not who she was." Her face told him nothing. "Eat and be welcome."

He did. It was the richest broth that he had tasted for many a day. He looked a question at her but she shook her head.

"When the manna fell from heaven they questioned it not," was all she would say.

He had another helping, while she began to talk about the afternoon.

"Your bow has not the spring to send an arrow very

far...good enough for poaching, maybe."

"Thou art a wily woman," he said. "What knowest thou of bowmen."

"Will Turner was the best. He could have taught you a thing or two. I can see no other one has done."

"I can shoot," he objected.

"Nay. Ye just pull the cord and let it go with a bang. Sometimes God does direct the arrow...sometimes not."

He had never seen her whole face crinkle in a laugh and a sparkle light her eyes as they did now.

"What meanest thou?"

"You have the strength for a stronger bow...the bow of a man."

"But not the money to buy one ...or the skill to make one."

"Reach up into the rafters....there," she pointed. "Pull that wad of sacking."

He stood up and could just reach it. He pulled and tugged until it fell into his arms.

"Before Will Turner died he said to put it there. 'Twill only be for a man who can reach to pull it down,' he said. "I have been waiting for you to grow to it."

He pared off the sacking to find a six foot bow of polished yew. She went to a chest and rummaged round to find a cord and showed him the miniature axe that had been used to shape the bow.

"Can ye string it?" she asked.

He knew what to do, but it took all his strength.

"Only just," she said, "only just. Now hold it and draw...Nay like this."

She took the bow. "Hold your right hand near your jaw and lean into the bow. And do it right. The villagers know this bow, and who made it. You must honour its maker. I will not let you have it otherwise."

For two weeks he tried, and asked, and tried again, until she was satisfied and let him take it to the butts on a Sunday afternoon.

He wasn't perfect, but at least he was started on the long road to be the best in his day. Will Turner would have been pleased.

It was a week day and Jacob was working on his own, cutting some chestnut stakes in a coppice when Roger came to him. "I have been trying to get you on your own," he said.

Jacob put his billhook down, not very sure of the reason for the visit.

"What have I done amiss now?"

"Nothing." Roger laughed. "It is just that I heard a rumour in the house that the knight from Tibberton is due back at the end of the week."

Jacob's memories of the knight's home-comings were not pleasant ones. He had purposely not seen Gill since he had moved to Edgmond. The long walk was not worth his bother, he decided.

"So?" he said.

"I had thought that it would be a venture to go on Sunday...if we can be sure that he is there."

Jacob pretended that he was not that interested.

"Have you ever been to one of them?" asked Roger.

"Once or twice."

"What about it then?"

Jacob, tired of the continual work and ready for some fun, nodded. "Right. But it may not be as good as the witches' coven."

"We'll chance it." Roger laughed. "Early on Sunday morning."

When he told the widow of the arrangements she asked,

"what are you wearing?"

He looked nonplussed. "What do you mean?"

"Do you think that Roger will be going in his Sunday smock which he wears among the wrestlers?"

"I had thought not of it."

She was quiet for a minute, then, "I know that you are a proud man, Too proud to appear in such a company in your customary clothes, even if your apparel is clean and tidy."

They eyed each other for a long moment, weighing each other up.

"I be no popinjay, nor wish to be one. Nor wish to appear what I am not."

"Nay, I would not wish to make you look...what you are not. When Will Turner was young, he served at the master's table when the occasion called for it. There is a doublet and joined together hose which we stored away, after he finished needing it."

He found himself afraid to say anything.

"Tis servant blue...not above your station. We can shorten one of your best smocks and fasten the hose points to it. The doublet may be a mite tight but wear it with the laces slack. Wear it open with a swagger. Oil your boots."

Early on Sunday morning was to their liking, a fair day with the heavy dew and a promise of a hot day when the mist had burned away. When Roger called for him he gave a long low whistle of surprise.

"By all the saints, you have a presence."

He turned to the widow. "I can just remember, a long time ago, when we were allowed to peep at the night time gatherings. There was a man who was similarly attired. He fitted the part well."

The widow smiled and looked a question.

Roger nodded towards Jacob.

“He does you credit,” he answered her.

“I am lucky to have another of the same ilk,” she said.

It helped to smooth Jacob’s stubbornness and they set off together querying what the day might hold for them. Their young legs, spurred on by the prospect ahead made light of the journey. They bypassed John’s old home and pressed on. By the time that they made Tibberton they could hear the sound of the gathering and were soon welcomed to break their fasts with the bounty laid out on the trestles.

Gill spied them and came to meet them, her tight fitting russet coloured gown flaring sharply out from the waist. Jacob hardly knew her, as her face was framed in the border of her veil which hid her hair and seemed to flow across her shoulders. Her eyes took a surprised glint as she recognised Jacob, but diplomatically cleared as she smiled to him.

“A stranger,” she said in a gracious voice, “with...?”

“This is Roger, son of Alleyn, from Edgmond,” he said with as much aplomb as he could muster.

“Tis well met,” she answered. “But I guessed so.”

She looked at Roger. “The knowledge of your hair has preceeded you.” And laughed in a low friendly banter. “Come, I must present you to Sir Richard”

They wended their way through the throng to find the Knight. To Jacob he seemed older than when he knew him first, broader of shoulder in his loose, startling white shirt and leather hose. He was fussing a war horse when they came to him.

“Your pardon my Lord.” said Gill, “two visitors from Edgmond to grace the occasion. Roger, son of Alleyn le Clerk, and a companion I knew long since. Jacob of the Caynton Moor.”

“How fares your father, Roger? Tis some time since we had the pleasure of meeting.” The stern face relaxed, taking years off his appearance. He gave a slight bow to Jacob. “I have seen you before. You grow apace...This campaign went well. Enjoy your day."

They left Gill with him, and joined in the festivities, mainly drinking and chaffing with the others. Some of the local Gentry arrived and joined the knight at his table.

Jacob, did not press his company on Gill but, several times, he saw her with Roger having a laugh together.

On the way home they recounted the food and the drink and the various spoils that the knight had on display.

"The warhorse is not for us," decided Roger. "but I could envy him his lesser mounts."

"If we had the time to ride them," said Jacob. "But it has been a day to remember.

They both agreed on that, although they did not share the same memories.

Jacob was changing. He did not realise that the meeting with Norma was a turning point in his life. Living with the widow had an unconscious effect on his outlook and being in daily touch with more people had awakened in him suggestions for his future.

He had been born into a family whose lifestyle had changed little for generations and knew that people were expected to stay in the various stations into which they were born. But that was all in the frustrations which had driven him on.

His initial concern had been thinking of making some money. Now he found that on this estate he had the prospect that, when he was old enough, and strong enough, he could claim some land to take the place of what he felt should have been his. A freemen with no land. But he had to be careful to keep his thoughts to himself.

Now that he lived in the village, he found that he could make more time for himself to explore the Manor lands which were available. He knew of the Brothers who farmed a neighbouring Manor for an Abbey and kept sheep for their wool. The land was similar to the Caynton lands but, below them, the valley was a mass of twisted oak thickets and scrub bushes, and goat willows and alders round the water pools and dangerous looking swamps.

Sometimes in a wet season the water covered the full width of the valley until it looked like a massive lake, until the water subsided and the grass was available again. He had heard that it was never used for sheep, as the marshland favoured foot rot, and also the fluke worm which lodged in the sheep's livers. The grass would, they said, clem a horse and dry a milk cow in a week. But he pricked up his ears when they said that oxen would do well on it, summer and winter.

He heard how the manor lands had been freed from the afforestation laws and was available to those who had the ability to clear or assart them, subject to an agreement to pay rent to the manor. With this in mind Jacob eyed the unwanted place. He had found a spot, where he went to poach the fish and snare the wildfowl, and had dug a hidden shelter in the hillside above the marsh. He was, by this time, sufficiently friendly with Atherton to make sure that enough of his plunder reached the Manor House to keep him out of trouble, especially fish for Ember days.

One night he was inspecting a warren near the Adeney Manor. There was a late moon, just appearing above Newborough, when he saw the ghost. His superstitious stomach gave a turn as he crossed himself with tingling fingers. Then the apparition was gone, silently floating into the tangle of trees in the valley. He had never ventured as far off his Manor before, as he was not sure how the monks would welcome trespassers, and was not acquainted with any paths through the morass.

He was still distressed when he reached the house.

"You look as if ye have seen a ghost," the widow said.

"I have," said Jacob.

She went very still. "Where have you been?"

"Down the marsh."

She let out a long low breath. "We talk not of that spirit," she said, crossing herself.

That was all she would say. in spite of him pressing her.

His curiosity was aroused and on the Sunday afternoon he left the usual gathering and went to have a look at the trees where he thought that the ghost had disappeared.

He found a narrow, scarcely visible opening through the undergrowth and, with heart in mouth and his feet following the tutoring of Atherton, quietly ventured along the path. On either side were dark brown muddy pools and the promise of what he knew could be bottomless morasses.

The sound came to him quietly through the thick twisted leafy branches and he stopped to reconnoitre. All was still. He suddenly realised that there was no sign of life, not even a scolding blackbird to tell of an intruder. A faint humming sound blended with the quietness.

He went on, using all the skill that he had learned on their poaching expeditions. Then he saw the hut, with a faint wisp of smoke eddying up from a fire. He felt relieved. A ghost with a fire?

She was sitting cross legged, her knees flat on the ground, her hands hanging loosely. She was sitting straight backed, her kirtle laces demurely done up to her throat. Her head veil, covering all her hair was severely tied back.

"Come," she said, without looking at him. "I had a feeling that someone saw me in my white gown. It must have been you. No one else has ever ventured along that path...except the monks. You should not have tried to find me. I am not for you." He said nothing. "I did expect you, although I have not met you."

"Who art thou?" he asked.

"Many years ago I came from an island in a warm sea with the Soldiers of the Cross. They brought three of us. I am the only one left. I visit the Ancellor house when they give the sign that I am required."

"What sign?"

"That is not for you to know. It is between me and them. This is a secret place, an island in a wilderness. But I am content. There is no place in the Ancellor house for a woman."

"But..."

"You were born at the harvest of the seed sown in well ploughed land. I know not your people but there is a free aura around you....and a fighter's mind behind your eyes. If you do harbour any antagonism there is much that you can do..if you harness it."

He felt frightened.

"Who art thou?" he asked again.

"I am known to many men. When the time is ripe I may reveal it all to thee, and of thyself. Now you have found me you must go. It would be better if you do not come again."

Her face became calm as her eyes glazed and she stared into space.

"Tell no one that you have been here, and bring no one here at your peril." A faint wordless humming note came from her half open lips. "Fare thee well Jacob," like an echo from a far off place.

He was back home before it struck him that it was odd that she should have known his name. For some reason he did not tell anybody, and he never heard her mentioned, except once when a witch was talked about. But they soon shut up when they saw that he was interested.

CHAPTER SEVEN

When he was nineteen, and counted as a full grown man, an event occurred which was to fashion the rest of his life. He was fallow ploughing on the demesne land when one of the villagers came running to say that a young bull was savaging a cow which was in season. When Jacob arrived on the scene he found a ring of villagers with staves and billhooks watching the bull trying to serve a cow which was obviously too big for him. In his frustration the bull had hooked the cow with his horns before the crowd had separated them.

Jacob had coveted it as a calf. It was just coming to its strength, dark red and square bodied on strong legs, with the beginning of a deep dewlap and incurved horns. As it stood alone, looking ready for any mischief, it was plain to Jacob that he had to do something quickly or he would lose it in recompense for the damage that it had done.

"Bring some more oxen," he yelled. "And get it in a crowd. Bring me some rope."

When they had the beast surrounded he pulled off his smock and quietly went among them talking all the time. He managed to get some of the bull's smell on his smock before he flipped it over its head as a blindfold, then quickly tied it in place with a halter and pulled it to a tree, talking quietly all the time. Meanwhile someone had fetched the bailiff.

"Tis a bad day." The bailiff said, shaking his head.

"Master. Tis not a deodan that we must take its life to pay for the error. Tis only a chattel that has been hurt. Tis not a surety that it must be killed. "

"Aye. Mayhap you are right." The Bailiff brightened at the thought and considered. "But is it a rogue?"

"Master, as you know, I know oxen," said Jacob. "We chose this one, and did not geld him, in order to use him some day. Twould be a pity to lose his stock. If I have him, I can tame him and use him to bring you more oxen than we need...and more to sell. And better quality than the old bull, who is too old now anyway...as you do know.

The bailiff looked surprised and then his desire for money made him wary.

"What do you mean?"

"If I can assart the land in the valley... which nobody else wants...but is ideal for oxen...to rear the young ones from his get, and I have every third calf for my wages, there will be enough oxen to work the demesne land, and extra beef to sell. And Newborough will need meat as it grows."

The bailiff walked away, as dealers do, and then turned back. "How will you do it?"

Jacob laughed. "Master I know not thy ways of doing things. Must I tell ye mine?"

The bailiff bridled at the cheek of the answer from an underling. "I can kill the bastard. We need some meat in the manor house."

It was Jacob's turn to be the dealer. "Twill be hard to present it to the Steward and the Auditors...with the old bull running out of time."

They eyed each other for a long minute while Jacob tried to appear sorry for the bailiff.

"Tame him and keep him," said the Bailiff at last. "We can use the old bull to cover the cows until the Auditors come in six months to take the estate assessment... then we will present your case." He turned and walked away.

All that night Jacob slept beside the miscreant, keeping it blindfolded, without feed or water. In the morning he asked for four men to hold a rope, two on either side. Then he fetched some water and let the bull drink until he had a bellyful and quietened down. Then, leading him with a halter rope, while the others steadied it on either side, he took it down to his poachers hide out and tied it to a tree and sent the others away.

When he told Mrs. Turner of his offer to the Bailiff she looked at him for a minute.

"What made you do it?"

"I have had it in mind for a while. It just came out. I don't know why."

"Twill be a long and busy summer," she told him. "And not much time for poaching...or aught else."

He took some food down to the bull and fed and watered it for three days, fussing it until he was satisfied that he had mastered it. It was his from then on.

His plan did not happen all at once. It only meant that he was one more precarious step towards the fulfilment of his ambitions. It also meant that he had talked himself into a predicament, as it entailed a great deal more work that he had expected.

The reeve was the first to have his say.

"Thou wilt now have the main charge of the oxen and the responsibility for supervising the services of the old bull. Which is my charge by right."

"So I will have both bulls?"

"Thou dost seem to know the oxen's welfare. See that thou dost not overwork the young one."

There had been an extended period of frost in the early Spring which had delayed the cultivations for the crops and meant that, in order to catch up with the work, all the available oxen and men had to be used when the weather was suitable. He had to do his stint in the cultivations to earn his day cash money, and the rest as best he could.

On the occasions when he managed to see Norma she was quite pleased at the way things had turned out.

"But you must be prepared in your mind for when the Auditors come. They are a devious lot in dealing with those who seek to better themselves. And my father also has to defend the manor against all those who wish to take from it."

"Tis always the same," said Jacob. "The ones who have, against the ones who have not. Even if they have to work hard for that which they do not have."

She laughed. "You are learning the way of using words, even if you have not been to school."

"The reeve cannot write but he knows all that doth transpire."

"The reeve is different. He has his position and land by the grant from the manor and guards his Lord's wishes. You have a chance to have...."

"What increase God doth give us, my mother used to say," he broke in.

She looked thoughtful but gave no suggestion of any solution to his problems. Not immediately, at any rate.

Norma, who had been brought up on the fringe of 'The Haves', knew that Jacob would be called on to deal with more difficulties than he was aware of. It also posed the question of her relationship with him.

Her tall, aloof father had tutored her in the ways of the Manor House where he had been brought up and she had accepted his guidance and his determination to hold to the French language, which was still the official one of the Government.

He was proud that he was the son of a French lady who was descended through the lower echelons of her Gentry family, and had been engaged as a tutor to the children of the Steward of the Manor who wished to preserve the French tongue which was still used by members of the upper class.

One season, a visiting French wool Stapler from the Continent came to buy the wool crop. As he enjoyed the hospitality of the house, he accepted the comfort of the maid who could speak his language. Alleyn, the fruit of the union, was allowed to grow up in the Manor House. He showed intelligence and acumen and was set to learn his letters with the parish priest. In due course he attended the better school in Newborough, the belief in his Norman breeding driving him to work at his studies and aim for the Clerks's role in the estate.

He had adored Norma, the slim embryo lady that his wife had given him and, in his secret way, had encouraged her in her book learning. With his access to the manor house he could see her as a lady's maid...at the very least, and laid his plans to keep her away from the drudgery of agricultural work. He had used her elder brothers' ability for figures and reading, and had been encouraged by his superiors to send them to attend the school in Newborough although the aim of the school was really to prepare men for service in the Church.

Norma's other brother, the red headed mischief, had willingly taken more than his share of the work on their croft and fortunately, had been a blood brother to her friend Jacob.

She had never been included in the discussions between her father and her brothers but had been allowed to listen to them. And she knew that any hint of an affiliation between Jacob and herself could cause enough trouble for him to lose any chance of his land, and his future. It was enough, at the time, to treat him as any other member of the Manor, no matter how good a workman he was.

Jacob never caught sight of the white lady on her ghostly errands again, although there was a strong compulsion in him to go and see her. He had worked out a roundabout hidden way through the trees, near to where she lived, only to find that she was indeed on a sort of an island, and he was forced to return to where he had started and use the path that he knew. This was indeed the only path leading into her hideaway.

One balmy day, with a whisper of wind blowing from the west, he decided that it was time that he went to see her. He took the path with caution and wondered at the heavy stillness in the air. When he reached the hut there was a deserted look about it. Unconsciously he softened his steps and crept nearer until he heard a murmur of voices coming from the open door. Perhaps she had a visitor. She had hinted that she gave words of advice and comfort at times to the Monks who needed her.

In no way abashed he edged nearer, but came to a halt as the voices became clearer.

"Oh Benedict, is this what you require?" she was saying.

"Yes, yes," replied a thickened voice.

"But it is against your orders for me to take you as nature intended women to do."

"And give me succour and comfort."

Jacob moved quietly to look in the door and came to a shocked stand still.

She was lying, facing away from him. She had taken off her kirtle and laid it as a blanket, her hips swelling bigger than Jacob had thought. Beyond her he could see the habit of one of the monks pulled up to the waist. He knew what they were doing and the thought of Gill came back to him. The herb lady laid back and pulled her smock further up, the man moving to cover her.

Jacob saw her turn her head and smile at him. A sudden

boiling inside him at her intimacy held him petrified, until he recovered in time to slip away, before the man in the Monk's robes came to himself.

He was amazed at the realisation that she had sensed his presence, and had enjoyed the thought of him watching her. There were many things that he did not know about this young old woman.

It was two weeks before he ventured to go back one Sunday afternoon, drawn by some force to the hovel. She was standing in her grey green long kirtle, a shawl, draping her shoulders, hung loosely open. Jacob noticed the swell of her full breasts, which he had not noticed before. Her skimpy veil showed her hair and her eyes had a welcome gleam. She spread her hands to greet him.

"I felt you coming," she said.

Now that he was there, remembering the last time, he felt tongue tied.

"Let us walk," she said, leading him past the house and into the woods. She obviously knew her way among the treacherous spots.

"I am a herb gatherer," she told him. "I eat no flesh of beast or bird. Christ's disciples were fishermen, so the Church doth allow us to use their harvest together with the fruits of the field."

"My mother had some stuffs that she used when we required them. But that is woman's work and I know not the ins and outs of these things. Except the wild garlic which you can smell."

She laughed. "That seems to be a world wide plant. Everybody is accustomed to using it where I come from. The knights have been used to it in their foods."

"My mother used the ash from the burnt bracken to make lye for soap," he said, trying to remember something to make it appear that he had some knowledge of the subject.

She pointed to some tall weeds, "I use that willow herb a lot, the roots and the leaves for wounds that they get from jousting. The feathery seeds make a good tow to carry with them for starting a fire with the steel spark." They wandered on until she stopped and reached under a bush to show him a small yellow flower." I use the root from this tormentil in due course to allay the toothache." She paused. He said nothing. "It was in the wood, gathering berries, that I first met the monk on a similar errand. The Brothers from Adeney are holy men and not allowed wives, as are also the Crusading Knights. Besides Benedict, the main brother comes as well."

"I have not seen the knights, and their workers keep to themselves," he said.

"They ride by night between their abodes."

They strolled back to the hut while she pointed out some of the herbs that she gathered. But he was more interested in what had happened the last time that he came, but she seemed to guide him away from such thoughts until they came to a spiny darkleaved bush.

"Tis the wonderful rosemary," she said. "It grows widely in the land I come from. It heals many things. Some of the knights swear that it helps them when their desire outreaches their ability."

She laughed but did not follow it up.

When it came the time to part she looked at him, her manner calm, voice quiet, as she said, "We were destined to meet, you and I...but only in passing. Take it not to heart. There is a woman waiting for thee, whether thou dost know it or not. She will know thy needs.

He was quiet as she continued, "Thou art a tempestuous man when thy desires are kindled. Treat her kindly, she will be to thee all that you will require...Fare thee well now."

She did not say 'till we meet again.'

The next time that he visited the island she had gone. The hut had been cleared of her belongings and stripped of the bundles of drying herbs. The only thing that she had left, lying in the middle of the floor, was a worn medal with a red cross etched into it.

Widow Turner had to admit to herself that she had treated Jacob almost like a son. Almost, that is, because there were certain areas in his life that she felt were none of her business. However the prospect that he might be leaving her, if he was to take the land that he wanted, made her ask him one day.

"How will you manage if you move down to the marsh?"

"I know not for sure. I was somewhat hasty with the bailiff."

"And if the Auditors are favourable? It is of necessity that you make a plan."

"Such as?" He looked the question.

"You will need to live on the land if you wish to claim it one day. And that means a house."

"I could make my cave bigger and get some help to build to it. It would suffice." He had thought it out.

"And live alone?" He was quiet at that suggestion. "You better sort out one of the village maidens in case you need a wife. The Steward will have to be approached for his permission." He looked away from her, indecision in every line of his body." The villagers are waiting to see how you fare with Norma."

She laughed at the look of surprise on his face.

"What know them of me and Norma?"

"In a village?...the gossips know everything...or fashion it to suit themselves. You and Norma...and her father." she pointed out. "You cannot hide anything in a village."

"She has said naught to me," he answered.

The widow looked hard at him but said nothing.

"And, anyway," he said. "I cannot say much until the determination is made by the Auditors and the Lord of the Manor.

"Leave it not too late," she counselled him.

It was, as the widow had said, a busy summer. Too busy to seem a long one, the weeks seemed to fly past. Work and bed and more work, and two tied up bulls to feed and use as the cows became receptive. And not much time to meet Norma. The widow's words had also made him very careful how he approached Norma, especially where they could be observed by the village people.

"You are getting high and mighty, now that you have the prospect of some land," Norma said one Sunday. "Too proud to associate with a humble kitchen maid?"

He was shaken out of his usual careful manner of hiding his thoughts.

"Tis not the reason," he denied.

"Then you have been avoiding me?" she accused him.

He realised that he had been outwitted and laughed.

"Thou art a woman of dealer's wiles," he said. "Tis...that widow Turner did say that the villagers be watching what will happen now, between thee and me...and y'r father."

"What should happen?" she asked, with a surprised innocent look in her eyes.

"If I get the herd, as I have already, and the marsh land to rear them on, Twill be needful that I live on it to claim it, and that doth mean a house."

She nodded her head. "And that will mean a woman to look after it...as the widow no doubt pointed out."

"Well...aye, she did."

"And...this woman...would not approve of me seeing you."

"What woman?"

"The one you will get to keep your house."

That was the moment that he would remember for the rest of his life. That all the planning and subterfuges and dissembling that he had put into getting what he wanted, was there in this seemingly helpless girl. And now she had backed him into a corner.

They looked at each other. Hard. Trying to read each others minds. She was the first to smile, she knew that she had won.

"I think we be two of a kind," he said. "Now what about your father? He be the man in the middle between me and the owners."

"I will have words with my mother. There is much for you and I to plan."

At the annual presentiment of the Estate Accounts to the Auditors he was allowed his say and felt the loneliness of a man trying to challenge the Aristocracy. Alleyn and the reeve made no objections...but they were loth to let the feudal system go, whatever their outward acceptance of the new conditions in the Nation. Every fifth calf was to be his, it was the best he could get; and the run of the marshes and what ground he managed to clear and assart; and help to make his cave into a one roomed hovel, built into the side of the hill and thatched with rushes from the Strine. He thought that he knew what he was doing, even if the auditors had not seen the possibilities.

It was even harder to get the wife that he wanted. Alleyn the Clerk would not sanction the marriage and the Steward over him could not, or would not, force him.

Jacob and Norma knew what they wanted.

"My mother accepts our marriage," Norma said one day. "She says that it would be a good risk...if we made up our minds to do things right and true."

"I would wish it to be different from my father and mother," said Jacob. "I liked it not that he was rough with her. But there will be hard work for you, ere we have what we want."

"You better bargain for the house before we do anything," she said. "After harvest the men will be free to do the building."

Norma made no mention of the strain that had arisen between her father and herself, nor the effort that her mother put into calming the troubled waters. Her brother Roger was all for the union. But then he knew Jacob better than anyone on the manor.

The house was completed, twenty four feet by eleven added on to his cave, wattle and daubed, the roof frame curving in to the ridge pole. The workmen had put all their skill into it as they admired Jacob and the way he tackled his work on the estate. The jealous ones were forced to hold their peace. Even the reeve did his best to forward the work. It cost Jacob nearly all his savings in a night of 'Building Ales' in Colley's Inn. But he had his house and the promise of some land. All he wanted now was a wife, and that meant Norma or no other.

Alleyn was still against a thing that he had planned to avoid. He wished that he had taken more steps to make sure that the friendship had been broken off a lot sooner, or indeed that, in the first place, he had refused Jacob the employment on the Estate.

He had come to admire his work and his application during the years that he had known him, and his courage in taking over the oxen herd. But as the husband of his daughter, and the thought of her being tied to manual work...he refused to consider it. He had been annoyed when Norma had moved into the kitchen without asking his permission. But his wife had judiciously pointed out that many of the Gentry houses were beginning to appoint women to the responsibility of Head Cook.

One day, Jacob was adding his day money to his growing savings when he came across the medal which the herbal lady had left behind. As he palmed it in his hand he could hear her say,

"There is a woman waiting for thee, whether thou dost know it or not. She doth know thy needs. Treat her kindly, she will serve thee well."

Widow Turner was growing old. Not that she had ever appeared young to Jacob, but in the passing of the years he had been in the habit of helping her with the heavy tasks in connection with the house and the garden. When he had told her of the plan to build the house she seemed pleased, but was just as pleased when he said that he would not be moving just yet.

Now that the thought of leaving her was in his mind he began to notice little things that made him worried. She had always given him the impression that she was indestructible, but now the signs of age were showing as she lost her active manner, and also in the constant references to Will Turner in her speech.

When he told her, as he thought he should, that he meant to marry Norma and move into the house, she sat still, very quiet until he thought that she had not heard him.

"I heard thee," she said, her voice suddenly taking the strength of their first meeting, and the accent of the peasants. "Twill not be long ere I cannot attend thee, as I should."

"Nay," said Jacob, taken aback at the unexpected thought. "We will visit thee anon and see to thy welfare."

"Be that as it may," was all that she would say.

Jacob had become more open in his meetings with Norma, but it brought its own perplexities. When he had first met her, he had compared her with his sisters...only better. Later when he saw her growing into a beautiful young woman he kept thinking of Gill and their times together. The thought of the risky consequences had made him try and keep away from the Clerk's daughter, but with little success. Now he was faced with the knowledge that she was the woman he wanted in his house, albeit on a better relationship than that of his parents. It would still be in a hovel such as he had been born into, far below the standard of a Clerk's home. Would the past be repeated?

Norma. on the other hand, knew what she wanted and how to get it, but dare not risk asking advice from any one.

They had not been able to see each other for two weeks and Jacob, against all regulations, called one night at the manor house and tempted her outside. The illicit meeting stirred the fighting spirit in both of them.

"I like not other people saying when and where we should meet," said Jacob.

She was surprised at his vehemence. "What do you want me to do?" she asked. She felt that she had to give him, as the man, the decision in the matter.

"We should be able to meet as we please."

"Why?" She asked, as innocently as possible.

"We have a house...and the chance of some land...we should be wed."

"Are you telling me?"

"What?" He sounded surprised.

"Or asking me?"

He stood for a space, dumfounded, and then it came to him and he laughed out loud. “By all the saints, you do surprise me at times...and myself too.” he added.

“My father will not allow it,” she said in such a way that he heard the disappointment.

They were quiet, thinking their own thoughts, while she waited. ‘not too long,’ she thought.

“There is a way,” he said. ‘but not one that I would wish to make trouble for you.”

“And if I was willing to take the risk?”

“Thou dost make it hard for a man.” He paused, then in a firm quiet voice. “I would give thee my hand in handfast and take thee as a man should.”

“And love?”

“I thought not of love. But if that is what I have felt for thee, these many years, then thou wilt have it for ever.”

They had never kissed. He had risked many things elsewhere but it was one of the things that he had never dared with her. They swayed together and he put his arms out to steady her but she slipped inside them. The rest of their world was forgotten as the fires of youth flared at the touch of their lips. He was amazed as he found her responding and gently loosed her.

“You were silly,” she laughed quietly, “...not to know. My father could not gainsay us then.”

Under the waxing hunter’s moon one night they pledged their troth by handfast and took each other as mates.

When they knew that their union was consummated they went, very humbly, to the Steward and disclosed their handfast, pleaded to be exempt from a Leywrite fine for their incontinence and offered to present themselves at the door of the church for the Parson’s blessing.

The Steward did not want to lose a good freeman who could make money for him, and he put a minimal price on the woman chattel that he was losing by marrying a freeman.

In a way Alleyn had no option. For all his dedication and the hidden determination of his own ambitions he was still tied to the customs of the manor. He wished again that he had listened to his doubts when he first took Jacob as a worker.

When his wife suggested that the future might turn out better than he had planned, it gave him some consolation, and he had enough training in hiding his thoughts from the world. The fact that his wife approved of his attitude was another source of comfort to him.

Widow Turner did not see them wed. Jacob found her wandering in the garden one night when he came home late from work.

"Will," she asked him, "where hast thou been? The meal be spoiled this last hour gone."

For the first time in his life Jacob felt feared. Gently he led her into the house and laid her on the bed, her eyes vacant and wandering. He wanted to go and find help but this was a private matter. He knew he was losing the only thing that, till then, he could have called his own. He held her hand as she wandered in her talk, slipping back into the idiom of her childhood, and slept. Then wakened to wander again through the years with Will. He grew cramped as the night chill entered his arms and legs but he never thought of moving.

As the cool grey dawn filtered into the cottage that was full of memories for both of them, she stirred.

"I'm coming, Will," she whispered in a long sigh.

Gently he slid his hands free and went outside to dry his eyes before he roused the neighbours in the next cottage.

CHAPTER EIGHT

In her father's eyes Norma was a daughter of the Manor. Although he was not of the real gentry Alleyn felt that, as he had been born into the Manor house, he was entitled to his standing over the villagers on the manor. Having accepted that the plans for the marriage were going forward, he had no intention of allowing her to wed without the ceremony that would show her above the common villagers.

Her mother also had her standards which she was determined to demonstrate to the rest of the village. A day was set which would give her time to organise the feast and all was prepared, except the weather. A favourite saying of the parson was that 'the sun doth shine on the righteous and the unrighteous', which allowed them all to guess which was which, and forget the sin which had brought the marriage about.

On the village green along from the church, the trestles were set up and the viands assembled. Alleyn had given a ewe which Maykin and his apprentice had been roasting from before daylight; Wheaten bread and lumps of cheese; the beginnings of the fruit harvest were there; cooked fish from the Mere and some dried herrings; all sorts of sweetmeats from the Steward's kitchen; two barrels of Colley's best brew; some wine set aside for the better quality guests. A body of minstrels coaxed up from Newborough at a cost of two pounds.

The evening before, the autumn sun had gone to bed behind the Wrekin in a promising rosy glow and, in the morning, had reappeared over Newborough to grace the day.

Jacob was not sure what he had let himself in for as he

had been forced to relinquish his comfortable smock for the day. In the flurry of preparation he had been measured for Gentry type joined- together hose of Kersey wool which he now wore, gartered at the knee. The village Cordwainer had made him a new set of round toed boots which were specially oiled for the occasion. He was pleased that they had been made with an eye to the future, strong and heavy soled.

For the first time in his life he had on a fine woven Lawn shirt and a tight fitting, lined Fustian doublet. Norma's mother had insisted.

"We will show the peasants that our daughter is marrying a man of substance," she had told him. "Store them well for the future."

He was pleased with his black felt hat. There would be some good wear in that.

Cleanshaven, proud of his newly oiled boots and his black felt hat, he squinted his eyes into the bright sunlight when he heard the commotion heralding Norma's arrival. He gasped at the sight of this woman who he did not recognise. She seemed to glide, her long gown brushing the grass which had been scythed close for the occasion, walking with an air of assurance.

He saw the rising hood with a silk gauze veil floating down over her shoulders, her face not yet in focus. Her gown, of some deep blue material, was kilted round her waist at the front to show the glistening lining, and at the turned up sleeve cuffs. He looked at her face above a pale muslin infill at her breast, where her kirtle was slashed to a deep V neck.

Suddenly she was there in front of him, her eyes a deep black brown in her pale face. She seemed to sense his wonderment and he saw the gleam of mischief as her eyes softened. She put her hand in his and they turned to the Parson who was waiting at the door of the church.

He hardly knew what he was saying as he repeated after

the Parson...."to haven and to holden, for fairer, for fouler, for better, for worser, for richer, for poorer, in sickness and in helthe, till death us do depart, if holichurch will it allow." Nor did he hear Norma's response to be "blithe and obedient in bed and in board, till death us do depart."

He marvelled that day at Norma's coolness as she moved among the company. Some of the Burgesses had come from Newborough, mixing with master workmen from neighbouring holdings. He surreptitiously loosened the lacing on his doublet but avoided the temptation of too much drink.

Jacob's mother and his two brothers and a sister were there, dressed as neatly as he had never seen them before. His mother excused his father's absence with a slight shrug of her shoulders, as much as to say,' you know how it is'.

Young Alleyn and Pierre had arrived the night before and wished them both well. Pierre, dark eyed and handsome, dressed in the latest London Merchant's fashion, loose jacket buttoned up to the neck, gathered at the waist by an ornate belt. The split sleeves, hanging loose allowed his arms to touch his sister's shoulders as he kissed her roundly on both cheeks. He looked at Jacob with a mischievous smile.

"Now, brother-in-law, you have the land, and a wife to boot. Your habit becomes you well. Bless you both."

Young Alleyn, as quiet and secretive as his father, shook Jacob's hand and bestowed a quiet peck on Norma's cheek.

Roger winked at his sister, punched Jacob on the shoulder, and gave them a gander and three geese wives to help them on their way.

Her father paid the Merchat fine of five shillings to the Manor. Three months income for the freedom of his daughter. For richer or poorer or better or worse, who could tell?

In the late afternoon, when the tables were nearly cleared and the jollifications were well under way, Jacob and his wife strolled quietly down to their house. A sudden swirl of returning fieldfares swept past them, their brown colour replacing the black of the swallows, who had left for other shores. A change in the life of them all.

And love in its fashion grew between them.

Norma was well aware of the results which followed the choice that she had made. She had taken note of the organisation of the Manor House and her father's house and had determined to do her best in the conditions which were now part of her man's life.

Carrying the baby was not easy for a sixteen year old who had not been accustomed to the heavy duties of the farm life. But she struggled on. She had achieved some of her ambitions; she had the man she wanted; and she had her freedom. Nevertheless she wanted both herself and Jacob to have a way of life which would give them a standard to which she had been accustomed, and a son to inherit the land when they had passed on.

Norma knew that her family had enjoyed the land, albeit as a perquisite in the custom of the manor. Any land which she and John might acquire would have to be won by their own efforts and be subject to rent, paid by cash or labour. Norma's mother, when she saw the choice that her daughter had made, in her quiet way had encouraged her in the alliance with Jacob, observing at the same time that she would have 'A hard row to hoe'.

When they were first married they were faced with a dilemma...two in fact. One, that they had taken on an unspecified stretch of farm land and two, an unspecified cattle herd. Both had possibilities for the future but the initial prospect meant that they were short of ready money, as the time spent on day work on the demesne for rent cut down the opportunity for the cash reward for day work. It also meant a slow return from the calves, whilst waiting for them to mature.

It was not that Jacob was foolhardy or a dreamer. He had been brought up in a hard school but had an unconscious acceptance of his own ability to deal with a situation and, provided he could see an advantage, was willing to take a chance on the outcome. He had good legs and a strong back and thought that would get him through any difficulties.

He had, as it so happened, a wife who understood him and played her part. Norma had tried to explain to Jacob the gulf which existed between the Gentry and themselves.

"They own the land from the King and everything that is on their land. They show it by their actions and their dress. There are some men who have made money, buy land from the Gentry, and try to act like them."

"And?"

"We will have land, and stock, by an age old manor custom. But not much ready cash for a long while. We will never be Gentry, but we will be a better class than the serfs and the peasant geburs. So long as God gives us health and strength we will prosper."

"But we will still be held by the customs of the manor?" he said. "The Church doth teach us that we may not seek to rise above our station."

They started out with a cow fresh in milk and a castrated bull calf, six chickens and a cockerel and a sow set to farrow in the Springtime. Jacob had made a straw beeskep when he was single and had come to a satisfactory arrangement with Atherton the gamekeeper about supplying fish from the meres and white meat conies for the Ember days. They had the three geese and a gander that Roger had given them. These were his own, but the original ox-herd belonged to the manor. The herd had been bred on the marsh land and knew the grazing patches but Norma had to herd them when John was on his manor work.

They managed to plough and sow two acres of wheat before the winter set in, sowing some rye beside it to mix with the wheat flour for bread. Jacob chose a promising piece of ground to break with the plough to allow the frost to moulder it, ready for sowing a crop of barley in the pring. Using changes of oxen, in order to keep them fresh for the extra work, they pushed themselves through all the daylight hours that God gave them, Norma driving the oxen while Jacob wrestled with the plough on the newly broken turf.

To Jacob and Norma food was their first priority. There was a drought in the Country the year they were married, so the harvest was poor and, as they had no land ploughed, they had to pay dear for their corn. In November, they reported to the Steward that one calf had 'unfortunately, broken a leg and died.' It was a well grown calf and, as it so happened, Jacob had managed to bleed it well, and was able to salt the meat. As he had been feeding it specially well beforehand, it was in good heart. It was a much needed and welcome supplement to the cheese, eggs, fish and rabbits. If there were any suspicions in the minds of the reeve or Alleyn, they were never mentioned.

Owing to a fierce storm, in the January before they were married, there were many trees blown down in the still thickly wooded manor, and the villagers were allowed to gather their share of firewood from the fallen timber. By giving some 'helpful' advice, Jacob was able to direct them to the ground he wished to clear for cropping, with a view to registering it. By astute herding of the bullocks he was able to break down some of the tangled growth under the trees on the edge of the marsh and compact the soil to prepare it for future use. It would be years before it was an accomplished fact but he had the brashness of youth allied to the cunning of experience.

Jacob had to take three bullocks to a butcher in Newborough and, as none of the dogs on the manor were trained for droving cattle, he decided to take them by himself. He thought that as they were fit-fat it would be an easy walk. Norma gave him some help to get them down the hill and over the Strine Ford and on to the road from Longford. He took them steady from then on but it was a muggy day, with the sweat hanging heavy, and the gad-flies a constant torment to all living creatures. Jacob, on his own and on foot, trying to be in two places at the same time as the fly-fractious beasts split up, was in a muck sweat by the time he had reached Newborough. When he neared the town some youths appeared, ready for any adventure. He gave them a shout and they willingly set about hazing the wanderers.

"We'll take them by the Drover's Road to the pound behind the Cock Inn," he told them. With much shouting and gleeful abandon they managed to get there.

"A good thing there were only three," said Jacob. "Thank thee kindly young sirs."

They went off laughing, looking for more mischief.

There was no money involved in the delivery so he and the butcher repaired to the Inn. The contents of the first flagon disappeared like mist in the morning sun. With the second one Jacob took his time and was introduced to a bright-eyed, slim little man whom he had seen in the tavern on other days.

Joby was a quiet man, whose manner suggested the quick active movements of a field mouse. Jacob noticed his long slim hands when they fondled the leathern ale jack.

"Did you bring the cattle with no help on such a day?" he queried with a wry smile.

"Tis so," Jacob nodded.

“You need a dog to do y’r running,” stated Joby.

“Tis well said. But we are governed by the Steward in the dogs we are allowed to have on the Manor.”

“Are ye good with animals?” asked Joby.

“Middlin’ so,” said Jacob in his wary bargaining manner.

“I do the animal doctoring round here,” went on Joby. “That is why I frequent this drovers’ meeting place....I do hate to lose one.”

“So?” asked Jacob.

“I have a litter of pups, but one will need fussing to rear, and I have not the time to give it.”

“And what of it?”

“It is got by a bull baiting dog out of a strong bitch. If reared and trained properly to quietness, mayhap it could herd gelded oxen,” was the suggestion.

“What ails it?”

“It was the last of the litter and came backwards road on...I had to help it out. It doth suck..but feebly.”

“I have no cash money,” said Jacob with a sigh.

“I know.”

“Know what?” asked Jacob in surprise.

“Your doings on the manor,” was the quiet reply, with a tone of sympathy but no recriminations. He laughed at Jacob’s surprise. “I make it my business to listen to the gossip which pertains to my work. I admire y’r choice to be with the animals and y’r pluck to take a chance with that young bull and the land. But pluck is not enough in this life.” Jacob shrugged his shoulders. Joby’s bright ferret eyes narrowed in speculation. “Take thou this runt. If ye rear it not..or it turns into a rogue with the bullocks, and you must kill it... at least it will have had a chance. I do not wish to end its days without it having one.”

Jacob thought about it. The upshot was he set off home

with, over his shoulder, a satchel holding the small whimpering pup with its eyes just open. When he reached home, he fed it, using a goose quill as a teat, whenever it asked for food, with Norma taking over when he was out working. As it grew bigger, he would carry it with him and tie it up as he worked, to accustom it to himself. As soon as it could run he started to train it to heel. It learned quickly that his voice and the leather strop meant what it said.

He let him have a cloth to worry, with the oxen smell on it. Then he kept it from him until he could tease him with it and let him bark at it without biting. It took some time to train its father's baiting disposition out of him but, after six concentrated months' training he had a dog big enough and pushing enough to tackle the oxen without nipping them. As the pup grew, its colour settled to a streaky grey and, when in full flight, he reminded Jacob of a badger. He named him Brock.

Brock was his dog and no one else's. He would even curl its lip at Norma but Jacob was pleased with the result of his training plus the bonus of getting him for nothing. Nevertheless, whenever he went to Newborough he made a point of calling at the Cock and setting up a quart of ale for Joby.

The prospect of a baby was another, although welcome, challenge to add to their determination of striving for the life that they planned for themselves. The long winter nights meant less work on the land and it allowed Jacob the time to make some furniture for the house and tools for outside work.

One night Jacob, wearied with the toil of the day, stretched out beside Norma and was quickly dropping off to sleep. She wakened him with her laughter.

"What be the matter now?" he wanted to know in frustration.

She laughed. “It’s a good thing we made this baby before we took the farm.”

“What meanest thou?”

“There doesn’t seem much chance of making one now...with all this work.”

The villagers had their neat cows for milk and grazed them on the upper moorland open communal field where the grass was more suitable for producing milk. The cows had to have a calf every year to keep them in milk and the villagers were willing to trade the calves against the bull’s service. It also saved them the feeding until the calf reached maturity. Jacob had all that in mind when he made his bargain.

Jacob’s plan, which he kept to himself, was to liberate more free land for himself. In order to carry out this land clearing operation he had to graze the existing grassland hard with as many oxen as he could. With this in mind he made a suggestion to the reeve.

“If the estate does not sell as many unfinished beasts as they usually do at killing time in the autumn, I could use the grass which has been squandered in other years”.

“Tis a thought,” agreed the reeve, “but thou knowest that we lost two good bullocks last year...and some every year for the past four years. Drowned in the winter bogs we reckoned.”

“Aye,” agreed Jacob, “one just before Christmas and one at the end of January. We sought high and low, but no sign of them. Hob Booth was the herdsman who counted them each day, was he not?”

“Aye. For the last six years.”

“Aye,” said Jacob nodding his head. “He was not overly pleased when I took the herd and told him that I would be doing it my way.”

“Well tis up to you. We better see Master Alleyn about

thy wishes."

The result was that Jacob had ten strong yearlings and fifteen heifers in calf to the young bull, and ten older stock. These were to be an off-herd to graze the meadows before shutting up time and then on to the marsh land, while the other oxen were spread between the villagers and the ploughmen.

It was not often that he went to the Lamb Inn but, when he did, he began to sense a certain amount of antagonism among the men and, especially at work, among the oxmen. He could not find anything to complain about until he lost one of the mature bullocks.

"Art sure?" he asked Norma when she reported one missing at an evening count.

"Of course I'm sure. There was a full count last night. But most of them were on their feet this morning, and some among the trees, so I didn't get a proper count this morning."

"Tis too late now to seek it in the dark. Was it one of the full grown stock?"

"Yes."

"Where were they lying last night?"

"Same place as usual. Why?"

It was not Jacob's nature to divulge half-formed theories.

"Oh nothing. Only last year the estate lost one about this time. We will say naught about it to anyone...for the time being."

She looked at him, waiting for more. But when he said naught, she left him to his own devices.

It was a quiet Christmas, the usual week's holiday from the manor work was taken up with work on their own holding.

"Tis usually a time for rest and jollification," said Jacob. "But there is much to do on our holding. What think you?"

"It is our first Christmas in our own home...on what will be our own land," she added. "Next year might be different."

Jacob laughed. It was the first time that Norma had seen him laugh for a while.

"We will make time for some rest," he said. "It would be a trial for you to walk to the village, in your condition, there and back in this weather, and the chores to do. I took my time off at the ploughing ales."

"That was your right as herdsman with the oxen."

"It did seem strange without you," he said remembering his father.

A flurry of snow in the beginning of the month made them plan for being snowed in, but most of it had lifted before Christmas, leaving the ground hard with frost. Norma had suggested that she might spend more time in the house and Jacob, worried about the child, agreed to it. It meant more work for him outside but, remembering his mother slipping on the ice, he assented to do it.

He had a surprise on Christmas Day when Norma asked him to go and tell her mother that everything was as it should be with them.

"Tarry not in the Lamb," she laughed when he left.

He was in a quandary to understand Norma's manner and it worried him. He told her mother that all was well, but that Norma did not want to risk the journey up to the village in the hard weather. Alleyn was not at home but, as Jacob neared his own house, he met him riding away from it.

"Good morrow, Master Jacob," said Alleyn. "A good Christmas to you...and my daughter."

"Thank you Master, I did go to take our good wishes to Mistress Agnes."

Alleyn, his face expressionless as always, nodded and heeled his pony to go on his way.

When Jacob arrived home he got one of the biggest surprises of his life. The table was set as he had never seen a table before, even at Widow Turner's. Two places set with pewter platters, which he did not know they possessed; a hunk of special cheese; two fish jellies; and two figures in some sort of paste. In the middle of it all was a bottle.

"My father brought a bottle of wine. He hopes that it suits your taste."

"Godstruth," said Jacob, "whew..."

He sat down, overcome with the surprise. "I am sorry." he said, "I met your father. He said naught of this."

She laughed. "It seems he says naught of a lot things which he thinks. Let us eat and be thankful. I have a capon all ready for us."

She came to him and looked him in the eye.

"Jacob," she said putting her hands on his shoulders and looking into his eyes, "we will not always be poor. Not the way you work. I learned the Gentry way of dining. Every Christmas we will have a feast such as they have. The rest of the year we will fare well on workman's victuals."

"When did you do all this?"

"When I pretended to be sickly."

"I have said it before. You are a devious woman."

CHAPTER NINE

Jacob was in trouble. And he knew it. He had lost one ox before Christmas, and did not know the reason, and Norma had just told him that there was another one missing from the morning count, and he did not have the time to make a search.

His biggest problem was that it was his nature to keep his thoughts to himself and then, when he had decided on a course of action, he wanted to carry it out on his own. His secondary consideration was, in this instance when he needed help, that he did not know who he could confide in, or what they would be prepared to do.

In the first place he had gambled on his physical ability to be able to shepherd a bigger herd than the Estate had ever asked the reeve to look after. Added to that, he had his other work on the estate to pay for the land that he had acquired. On his own land, after the frost gave up, they had managed to cross-plough and sow an extra two acres of barley on top of the ground in the spring. This gave them, come harvest, the promise of some seed for the next year, and malt for the necessary ale.

After the loss of the first ox, he had not explained anything to Norma, but they had worked out a system that Norma would go out at daybreak to make her count before he went off to the demesne.

"Bugger it," he said. "They can manage without me today. If the reeve sends to know where I am, then we will acquaint him of the circumstances."

The night before, Brock who was tied up outside, had wakened them with an excited barking. Jacob had gone outside but had not been able to see, or hear, anything. At daybreak Norma had gone to check the oxen while Jacob was having something to eat, and now they had a problem to solve.

"Is it one of the strong ones?"

"Yes."

"Drive not the rest of cattle down on to the marsh. Get something to eat and come and meet me down there. We will examine the land to see what signs we can find. Tis no good leaving it till later when the others will trample all over the place."

Before she came down to him he had counted all the stock, including the ones who had moved into the marsh. Pressing on he found a place where the mark of the oxhoofs were accompanied by one or two men's footprints on muddy patches. He showed them to her when she arrived.

"Go back to the house and do your chores," he told her. "I will follow these footsteps and determine what went on."

"Is it a man then?"

He nodded. "Or two. They must be well known to the oxen, to be able to take one out so quietly."

She looked her astonishment. "You knew all along?"

"I thought so. But thoughts are no use in these circumstances. Go now. I will find out what I can."

"Where will they take it?"

"Either along the Adeney marshes. Which I do not suppose. Or over the Long Ford. Which they did not do the last time. Or along the Edgmond marshes to Newborough."

"Guard your steps," she said and left him.

He went back to the footsteps that he had found and carefully followed the tracks in the wet ground. He came to a pool where the spoor disappeared and stood, while he considered. He listened with his mind to the things said and hinted, in the Lamb and elsewhere, which he had disregarded at the time.

'It was quite true', as they had said, 'that he had more animals to shepherd than in other years.' It was quite true, as the man had said in a sly way, 'that there was more water about than in other years.' The expected snow had fallen as rain, even the Strine was flowing deeper than might be expected. 'You might even lose more than usual,' the man had said. Had there been a veiled threat in the innocent sympathy.

The pool was really an inroad from a bigger stretch of water which came from the valley, and had seeped into a stand of willows. They could have gone any of three ways and where would they leave the water? Some instinct made him head for a gap in the half submerged bushes. He prodded with his staff to find the depth and edged his way across the waters, letting his glance rove round, seeking he knew not what. There was a mass of brambles to one side which made him look again, and swear.

There was more swearing as the thorns caught at his clothes and jagged at his legs before he found what he was looking for. Half a horn, cut across above the growing point, and thrown into the bush where it would not be found until springtime, if even then. It did not take him long to find the other one which had penetrated the thicket.

'This is a butcher's job and no mistake,' he reckoned, 'to make it easier to lead them through the thickets in the dark.'

Soaking wet and cold, he felt the surge of hate through his body. He suddenly knew how to deal with the situation, now that he had something definite to go on.

Norma was speechless when he clashed the horns down on the floor and, bending down he stripped the wet smock over his head.

"We have the sods now," he laughed.

"How?"

"Atherton and I know a thing or two which will scare hell out of the thieving swine."

"Why Atherton?" She sounded suspicious.

"Atherton?" He looked shamefaced."....Oh...eh....never mind. There may be one or two things that you may not know."

She did not like it, but had enough sense to bide her time, laughing inside at his naivety.

Jacob went to see the reeve that night to make a fictitious explanation for his absence from work that day, and then went to the Lamb for a drink. He hoped to see Atherton his crony, who had taken the place of his father the gamekeeper, who was stiffening up with arthritis.

It was not considered right for a Manor man to be friendly with the representative of the owners, especially the gamekeeper. So Jacob never professed any outward friendship in front of the villagers, but he lingered by Atherton's side and in a soft voice whispered, "I may see thee anon in a quiet place." Atherton flickered an eyelid and that was all.

"Hast Norma let thee off the leash tonight?" jibed one wag.

"Nay. I had to see the reeve and must be returning home. She doth keep a watch on me to keep me from mischief."

He swallowed his drink and his eyes flickered a question at Atherton and received a hidden yes.

He had barely reached home and asked Norma to look out the best ale when a knock came to the door. Jacob took the candle lamp and shaded it from the door. "Open it," he said to Norma. "Tis Atherton." It was. "Pour one for yourself," he said to Norma who had set them up. "This is no women's work. But you are in it. So have your say, which we will attend to."

"What is it all about?" Both Atherton and Norma wanted to know.

"When I took over the oxen herd, I wanted to do it all by myself, because I had not the money to pay Hob Booth to waste his time herding...and have him poking his nose into my affairs. We lost a bullock before Christmas. We did you know," he answered Atherton's look of surprise. "Well I said naught to the Estate because it seemed that it was a regular thing these last years past. And they seemed to accept the reasons then."

"And you found not anything that time?" said Atherton.

"No. The bullocks were scattered in the marsh before I found them," said Norma, "covering any trace of anything."

"Then we lost one last night." said Jacob.

" 'ods blood!" said Atherton.

"Well, we had made our plan, so I went down for a look and found where it had gone. And two half horns in the bushes. With two men, I think."

He trailed the horns out to let Atherton have a look.

Atherton was too surprised to swear this time.

"Now." Jacob continued. "The bullocks must have been acquainted with one of these men, or they would have been disturbed. He could slip a halter on one and they could lead him off. Probably pick a fit one."

"Who?"

"I think Hob Booth. He has been in charge all these years. I reckon he is in league with one of the butchers in Newborough. He picks it, helps them collect it, this time a good butcher's saw to get the horns off above the growing point, and through the bushes with less hindrance."

They were both silent and then Norma said, "He could have tied it up, out of sight in the afternoon, and then they could collect it."

"No," said Jacob, "I think not. He must meet them at night and leave them when they are on their way. And, maybe, have his money in his hand."

"He was not in the Lamb last night," said Atherton. "I always check the rogues. When they be absent I go to search the spinneys. But he was not there."

"Other years," explained Jacob, "the bullocks fatten up quickly on the dead marshgrass. So there are in fine fettle till the end of January. After that they loose some fitness but will still be in fair nick for when the grass comes again in spring. That is without feeding them any hay." They agreed with that. "Now." He looked at them while he decided to speak his mind. "If Hob sees that I have done him out of his ill-gotten money. And it looks as if it is the end of his nefarious doings and he seeks to do me real harm, then he must come for another one before the end of this moon."

Norma looked at Atherton. "What I guess in my mind, I will not say," she said. "But. If my man chooses you to help him in this venture, then I am with you both." She lifted the jug and reached over to fill his tankard.

Atherton's laugh gurgled in his throat. "My lady," he answered lifting his tankard, "My respects to the lady he chose."

They settled down to make plans to thwart any likely raid in the near future. Atherton would keep watch on Hob; Norma would drive the younger stock on to the higher ground and leave the bullocks in a handy position for the thieves; they would take notice of the moon and rely on Brock to give the alarm.

Several nights passed in quietness, which only added to the tenseness between Jacob and Norma. At work he kept away from Hob in case he showed his suspicion. After all he might not take the bait. But, with Jacob not openly admitting his losses, it was a good bet that Hob's greed would get the better of him.

One night they had decided to retire, deciding that nothing was going to happen, when Brock started his alarm.

"Shade the lamp from the doorway till I get out," ordered Jacob. "I will find them and follow them. Please God, Atherton is at hand."

He belted his smock and hung his knife, grabbed his staff and slipped out the door. The moon was behind him, shrouded in a cloud but his eyesight soon became accustomed to the dimness. Striking along the higher ground parallel to the way the robbers would have to take for Newborough, he caught sight of a flash of white on the bullocks belly. One man was hauling on a lead rope while another behind goaded for all he was worth. It looked as if they were keeping out of the trees, seeking a faster journey on the cleared ground.

He picked a spot for an ambush where they would have to pass through some scrub and waited impatiently. He saw that it was Hob on the halter rope, and in a rage he jumped out bringing his staff down aiming for the head. Hob checked but the blow took him on the shoulder bringing forth a yell as the bullock stopped. Jacob was lifting for another strike when the other man drove forward with his goad and Jacob felt the spike furrow along his ribs. He doubled up but still felt a club as it smashed against his head.

All was quiet when he came to. He shook his head to move the darkness from his eyes and winced at the pain in his chest. Gradually he got to his hands and knees but slumped again. He tried to swear but his chest was too tight. He had to do something. Summoning his strength he groped around for his staff and managed to stand. It was a long and painful stumble to the house.

Norma was shocked to see him. "What happened?"

"I know not. The sky did fall upon me. There must

have been another man behind me which I knew not."

"Quiet then until I bind you up."

When she had composed him, and given him some brandy from her secret store, they tried to figure out what might have happened and the outcome of it.

He couldn't laugh for the pain in his ribs, but his smile said a lot. "Hob will have some explaining to do, on his sore shoulder."

"I must do my chores," decided Norma. "Let the oxen find their own way."

They were sitting together in the late morning, Jacob chafing at the loss of the bullock and his inability to do anything, when they heard a shout. "Ho the house."

Norma went to open the door and Atherton strode through the opening. "Well met," he laughed. "ByourLady, what ails thee?" when he saw Jacob.

"I know not, where were you?"

"Ah., tis a long story." They waited while Norma poured some ale. "Well, tis like this," said Atherton when he had lifted the tankard to Norma and taken a mouthful. "I knew Hob was on to something when he slipped out of the Inn, and I knew that thou wouldst get wind of his doings at thy end." He paused for effect. "So...I positioned myself on the way they must take to the town. I heard the fight and then these two men came in sight driving this bullock as if all the devils of hell were after them." They waited. "Well. I had found out... never mind how. That they might be taking it to one of the sheds in the Hoyles below the bridge. So...I went hot foot to the Watch in Newborough and we apprehended them when they arrived."

"Tis a right story," said Norma. "Here. I found some brandy."

"Tis a grand tale. Have you seen Hob?" asked Jacob.

"Was he in on it? Nay I have not been to the village.

I came straight along the Strine."

"He will be marked by my staff, the two faced swine. I thought not of another sod behind my back."

"They will fetch him down to the lock-up to await the justice," said Atherton.

"And the bullock?"

"Twill be sold in the market. And the money go to the herd. Ye will have to tell of the others, and see how it transpires."

And it was so. Hob was hanged on Gallows Bank on the Newborough marsh. The other two, no doubt with the collusion of the Inn keepers who had hatched the plot, managed to escape and lodged themselves in the Church, claiming the Laws of Sanctuary. They confessed to their obvious error and were arraigned to travel to Dover, the nearest port of call, and, as was the law at that time, banished from the kingdom for ever. It was a great story and revived the tale of Jacob's feat with the young bull. It soon passed from his mind as other things came to worry him. Norma was nearing her time.

Jacob was busy with the oxen calving when he fetched Meg the mid-wife. He had been worried about Norma, whether she would manage, but Meg was there to see that all would be well, so he left it to her. She had a good name on the manor and had often chided him in her rough way when he was younger, to make sure that he did not cause any work for her among the unmarried girls.

"Get ye gone," she had told him. "Ye be the best there is wi' the oxen. Leave Norma wi me. My work is wi' the women. I'll see she comes to no harm."

But he was still in two minds. Norma's family had always been treated by the villagers as if she was lower Gentry but she had, without grumbling, taken her fair share of the peasant's work since they were married. At the beginning, he had made a promise to himself that he would act differently to Norma from that of his father to his mother. If, he thought, 'this baby be a boy I will determine that he gets a different upbringing from mine.' The last two days with Norma's pains had been long days and a worry on his mind.

But the oxen calves meant money for both him and Norma and he had to make sure of their being born. and the last straw which made him annoyed with himself, was when he found that it looked as if he had trouble with a cow. He had been busy and had taken a chance that the calving would be normal with a cow having her third calf. Now he could see that he had trouble.

Norma, in the truckle bed where Meg had laid her after the efforts on the birthing stool, said not a word but stretched out her hands to her firstborn. The sweat was still damp on her face, stark white against the black hair spread across the woman's birthing pillow,

"He hath taken a long time to make up his mind to be with us." said neighbour Groves, Meg's helper, while she raked the peat fire turves to keep the flame alive without the smoke.

Meg kept her thoughts to herself but she had been worried at the length of the labour. The child was what the villagers called a barley baby, born well inside the expected term after marriage. And Norma was only sixteen years and not too wide besides. She had seen many a stillborn babe or weak bairn die after a birth such as this one.

She busied herself with her work of tidying the room. The bed was at the end of the room away from the door, which had the top half open to let in the moonlight and some air. She fetched some clean linen from a wooden chest and piled the soiled sheets ready for cleaning in the morning, resetting the trestle table with the wooden platters for a meal.

This boy, Meg guessed, would live to make more bairns. But she would not be there to see them into the world like she had done with his mother, when she had been a slip of a lass learning her trade from her own mother.

"He will be a fighter," she assured Norma, "the red haired little ox. Ye took a chance when ye made him. But ye will be the stronger for it, I promise ye... if we watch y'r goings. And rear y'r son... if only for the sake of Jacob, "she added.

Even as she spoke of him, he was swearing and sweating as he made sure of delivering a calf with the least damage to one of his best kine.

The cow had broken the waters in the early afternoon and, with the two front feet showing, he had left her to the natural way of it. By moon up she was no further forward and by the time he had haltered her and tied her up to find the trouble, her passage was beginning to dry. All he could find, with his long arm inside her, was a solid mass of body and no head at the top of the calf's legs.

He had to walk nearly a mile, there and back, to find two helpers and now, with the cords looped on the calf's front legs, and the men gently pulling, he was inching his fingers along the bent-backed neck and over the forehead of the calf. He was a broad man with arms that could send an arrow two hundred paces to the clout with the best of his peers at the butts. But now, with the force of the contractions, his arm felt paralysed and near the end of his strength. He gritted his teeth and stretched some more inside the passage and felt the flood of relief surge through him as he found the nose of the calf. He worked the cord noose off his thumb and round the nose and relaxed.

Summoning his strength, he pushed the calf's brisket back and, pulling the cord with his left hand, he brought the calf's head forward to its natural position between the fore-legs.

"Now then take y'r time and pull steady when I say so," he told the other two. "I shall guide the head atween the legs and we will have the little bugger out in no time. Please God its alive."

The cow, sensing his willingness to help her, had quietened down in her exhaustion. Now, when the strain began she started to move and nearly wrenched his shoulder out of its socket.

"Come on ye great pillock," he groaned. "Tis nearly there "

A slithering, walloping avalanche and the calf lay in a heap on the grass. Jacob was at it in a quick movement to clean its mouth and nose of the caul and calving juice and, gulping his lungs full of air, he blew it down the calf's throat. Then, windmilling its front legs, he forced the calf back from the brink of death. At last, a tremor through its limbs and a sneeze, rewarded his efforts and he knew that he had won.

"Stand back and guard y'rself," he said to his helpers as he dragged the calf to the cow's head to let her smell it.

He took the drawstrings from the calf's legs and nose. Watching for the sweep of the yard wide horns, he quietly loosed the tethering cord and pulled the slipknot on the cow's halter and stepped quickly away. A new calved cow is more dangerous than a bull, he knew. She was too busy nosing and licking the calf to bother with him, so he bethought himself of the blood and grease on his bare body, and the throb in his arm as the circulation came back to its steady flow.

"Thanks to both of you," he said.

"Y've done it again," they said.

"Aye. I have not lost one yet.... You best have y'r rest."

A whisper of wind across his shoulders made him shiver. The stars in the blue black sky blazed in the frosty air.

"A water frost, it looks like," he said.

"Aye," they agreed. "But twill not be long now to sun up."

"There'll be a gallon for ye both at the Old Lamb."

"Thank thee Master Jacob. Fare thee well."

The cow had settled to a steady cleaning of the calf. Her brain, clearing from the excitement of her labour, responded to his known voice as he checked that the calf was a heifer.

"The chance of many more, please God," he said.

It flopped about on the grass as the strength grew in its legs, its brown pelt still black wet from the calving juice. Instinctively it headed for the beastings in the udder which would mark it by the smell in its tail end for its mother to recognise.

"I'll have some o' that in the morning," laughed Jacob. "for some custard."

As he stretched the ease back into his limbs he remembered Norma. It had been a long two days since the pains had started. He could usually foretell to an hour, by feeling the softening calving strings, when a calf should be born, but he knew not anything about women... about childbed anyway, he admitted. He knew not what he felt about Norma except that she was his woman, had been since she was five years old.

But he trusted Meg in spite of her looking old and wrinkled and dry and tough as the leather they tanned from the bullock hides. 'She be well past the fun of getting them but she do know the way of making sure they're born,' he laughed to himself.

When Jacob arrived at the house, he strode straight to the bed and took Norma's hand in his own, marvelling at the softness and lack of strength in it. She had never appeared to him as a soft woman. Their life was one of constant effort, even the rest periods were filled with various activities. They were well matched and content, but outward sentiment was not a conscious part of their commitment.

Seeing his surprise, she laughed. "I shall be all right by tomorrow. Fear not," she assured him.

"I never questioned you otherwise," he said. "It doth seem strange to see you like this."

He turned to Meg. "Will she be well?"

"Aye Master Jacob. A good, but tiresome birth...your son," she added, handing him a little bundle of clothes.

Jacob looked at his hands, toughened from work and still soiled from the calving. Gingerly he took what felt to his strength, like a bag of feathers. He knew the thrill from a new born living animal, but he was used to the kicking and striving of the calves. He was scared that he would drop this helpless part of himself.

"We shall have to call ye father Jacob now," laughed Meg.

He looked from Meg to Norma, a flush of relief coursing through him. As Norma looked at him, words and feelings, not often expressed, passed between them.

As if ashamed of showing any softness in front of Meg, Jacob laughed. "Tis been a great night. A boy and a heifer calf into the bargain."

"We will call him John," he told Norma, "that was my first name. When my younger brother was born, and would be my father's heir, he was called John and I was given the name John Jacob. So Jacob I became, Jacob the herdsman. Now that we have this holding, Jacob o' the Marsh most men call me."

CHAPTER TEN

Norma, lay on her bed and gazed at the bare smoke stained covering which sheltered her from the storms of summer and the snows of winter. She felt that it was the first time since she married that she was able to pause and consider what she had done. She had accepted the house, without comparing it to the one that she had been brought up in. Now, in her enforced idleness, she began to notice her circumstances.

The low slung bed, on a rudimentary wood frame, was in the cave end of the house, windowless and snug, the earth walls smoothed and limewashed. The smoke, from the fire on its iron plate, eased its way through the rush thatching at the far end away from the bed. The door to the outside, in the main part of the house, usually had the top half full open to let in the Spring air. Two holes in the wall for windows were wood shuttered to keep out the rain or the mist which came out of the waterlogged valley. In the summer they would be replaced by a frame with a sheepskin stretched on the wood. The pelt had been well scraped, by both Jacob and herself in the long winter evenings to give a translucent light in the dimness.

Somewhere from the marshes came a curlew's questing cry and the strident boasting of a barn cock, outside the door, stirred her to ask.

"Have I done right, Meg?"

She felt strangely listless and empty and useless, lying in a bed in the middle of the day.

"Thou wilt not know that, until ye do lie on thy death bed," laughed Meg, standing with arms strutted on her broad hips. If she had any misgivings about the results of the decisions in her own life she made a rule about hiding them, and showing only her ability to reassure those in her charge.

"What ails ye?" she asked. "Just because ye have some time to lie abed and think, instead of busying thyself from morn till night."

"This seems the end of something Meg. Something that I had planned for. Did I do right?... I lie and wonder. Lying in this bed. In this ...in this hovel."

"Tis not the end mistress. Tis the beginning ." Meg looked round the plain white plastered walls, the darkened wooden uprights and cross pieces, up to the cruck beams reaching to the ridge pole. "Tis not a hovel mistress. There be much to be done right enough. But tis a home. A home for thee and thy two men. And, in a day or two, when y'r strength returns..." She left the suggestion to take root and flower as she caught Norma's glance at the rude cradle with the swaddling boy lying quiet. "I brought you into the world." Meg said in her determined way. "What did ye expect to make between thyselves? Ye panicked methinks, and the firstborn is often a tardy coming. Do ye regret leaving y'r way of a lady in the big house?...In service," she added.

The sly inference was not lost on Norma. As Meg waited for her answer, Norma considered the implications.

She knew that she had been a wilful child, inheriting her father's determination, if not his guileful ambition. From her mother she had inherited the robust agrarian, down to earth outlook of the Saxon settlers. From her mother, she had learned the practical task of running a villein home and had taken her share of the woman's work.

"Is it any better being a slave in a hovel than a slave in a manor house?" she asked, emphasizing the derogatory word.

"Ye be a free woman now, and no slave as well ye know, now thou art married to a free man...and planned it."

Norma tried to deny that. "What do you mean I planned it? What do you know? Are you a witch as all women say?"

"Nay. I am no witch. My mother, God rest her soul, may hap was one, as near as made no difference. Albeit a white one if that be so."

"In what way?"

"She knew the numbers and the stars in their goings, and could tell when the seed sowing was for the best, and who was to marry and what would be their humour in their way of living. She told me that ye two would mate but of marrying she said naught."

Norma coloured as she felt the flush course throughout her body.

"We made a plan to marry," she excused herself.

Meg drew up a settle and sat down. "Maybe so. But that twas after."

"After what?"

"After thou didst leave the guidance of y'r father. Ye were meant to be a Seamstress and Broderer and learn to nurse the children of y'r master. Like the mother of y'r father."

Norma looked surprised, as well she might. "Who knows about that?"

"No one else, that I know of." Meg shook her head.

Norma defended herself. "My mother taught me how to cook and bake bread and make cheese and butter. And I learned the sweetmeats of the Gentry table, and the viands for their feasts. That seemed of much more importance...."

"To the wife of a master oxherd?" suggested Meg.

"At the time I thought not of it," lied Norma.

For she had planned, and very carefully at that.

Meg rose up from the settle and went to the fire. "Tis time for some broth to get thy strength back.' She pulled the swee round to reach the pot and ladled some liquid into a trencher. “Ye best make some milk for y’r little one. A wet nurse is not for thee. Sit up and help thyself, I have some tasks to busy myself with.”

She went outside, drinking in the clear tangy air of the May morning. Somewhere, the ringing cry of a lamb for its breakfast was answered by a throaty call from its mother. The early pre-dawn chorus was beginning to stir all around her. Mistress Groves came sloshing back with a bucket from the spring, her smock dragging in the frost-wet grass. “Tis the promise of a good day methinks,” she said in passing.

“Aye,” answered Meg. “A better Spring than last year, if it please God. With no rain till July, and then more than we could manage at harvest.”

Meg smoothed the rolled up sleeves of her kirtle down to the wrist and started to lace them. She watched the stocky form of Groves as she swung the bucket in front of her to edge through the doorway. ‘A kindly soul,’ she thought. ’Tis a pity that she hath only two girls of her own to show for her six attempts.’ It had left her with a shapeless body but no bitterness.

Meg followed her into the house and began to lay out the wooden platters and butter and cheese and bread. She added some cold meat in case Jacob was hungry for it. She wondered how he was managing.

As Norma supped the thick potage she thought of the years before the hand-fast and the months since discovering the surety of the expected child. She realised that, as a youngster, she had thought that she knew her own mind. But during the last few weeks a doubt had crept into her reckoning. Jacob was a busy man who put the needs of his animals high on his list of importance. She had accepted that, so long as she had the strength to carry out the many and varied tasks that were her lot. But, in the frustration of her present weakness, she began to rue the path that she had chosen.

She had heard the gossip, when working in the kitchen, about how men neglected their wives after they were married. She remembered the terrible differences of opinion between Jacob and herself when they were young; how pigheaded he had been when he wanted to go off with the other lads and refused to allow her to accompany them; the arguments, when she was at school, of how he despised her book learning; how he complained about her brothers training to be the people who lived soft lives.

Norma reached over to put the plate away, feeling better for the activity of eating and the comfort of the warm liquid.

"Thanks, Meg. That was good."

"It doth happen often among women in childbed to feel as you do. Even amongst our common sort sometimes. But Mistress Penelope refused her child... and her husband." Meg tried to comfort her.

"When was that?"

"Before you entered service."

"What happened.?"

"The girl baby was put to a wet nurse. And then, can ye remember her being sent to her aunt in Chester and leaving the baby behind?" asked Meg.

"And Master Martin went to the wars?"

"Aye. And, no doubt, fathered a few bastards on the Continent." Meg laughed.

There was a silence while a thought stirred Norma's mind. At last she said. "Meg."

"Aye?"

"Do you remember Polly the daughter of the Cordwainer?"

"What about her?" A sharp counter question.

"She had a baby."

"Ye were but new in the kitchen then." Meg objected.

"I heard the gossip."

Meg was still and silent but she kept her gaze steady on Norma. "What was said?"

"The rumour was that Jacob the young herdsman was the father," ventured Norma, a suggestion of a question in the answer.

"Will of the Pool did marry her."

"Will of the Pool bought her to take the place of his dead wife. He was too old to get another otherwise," said Norma scathingly.

Meg neither agreed nor denied it.

"Thou wert but thirteen summers and knew nought of such things."

Norma laughed. It sounded shrill in the tense silence.

"You know these things," she said. "Was Jacob the father? He was man enough."

"Did ye not ask him?".

"No."

"Did ye think that he was?" Meg was curious.

"I did wonder," said Norma, "but he was my man. In service I was not able to see him as we had done before... And Polly was always ready for anybody." Norma tried to find an excuse.

Meg. quick to take the chance to change the thread of the conversation said. "She was ready for Will Pool in his widowhood and he was ready for her. It mattered not who got who. He paid the Leywrite fine to the manor and she had a shelter that no one else would give her. It worked out well for them both."

Norma let out a long shuddering sigh and put her face in her hands. Meg rose and placed her arm round Norma.

"After all these years ye did keep y'r doubt and then

began to doubt y'rself? It was not Jacob, Mistress," she assured her.

"I thank you for telling me." Norma lay back on the pillow.

It was true she had often thought about the gossip. But, if it had been Jacob, she had accepted that it had all ended tidy for everybody.

"Tis time to bathe and feed y'r lad," said Meg as she picked up the bundle, crossed with bandages to hold the swaddling wraps, a little face screwed up like a mouse peeping out from under a grass divot.

"He be a quiet one, that man of thine," she added. "He would only have laughed if ye had asked him."

"He says little about which way he thinks," agreed Norma.

"He does his work and knows that ye can do thine. He could never talk to his mother, but some day he will talk to thee. And then ye must listen, not to what he doth say but what he says not."

Norma looked at the little face attacking her breast and felt the strength of purpose stirring in her again. She stroked his back and arms while Meg looked on.

Meg kept Norma in her bed until the third day.

"I must be about my business, Meg." Norma had argued. "I'm no lady to be cossetted."

"Ye ought to be well enough to do much by now, as is the custom of our station. But thy labour hath been hard and there are many years of work before ye. I will remain here for a week," Meg told her.

"There is so much that I have been in the habit of doing," complained Norma.

"We will send Mistress Groves away. Jacob can do the outside chores and I will send Peg Little to aid you, till y'r full strength returns."

No one argued with Meg when she took charge. She had given more time and care to Norma than she would have done, but Alleyn was The Clerk, and well liked besides, and she was not going to risk his displeasure by treating his daughter in an ordinary fashion.

Norma had risen, in the mornings, to take her son from Meg and undo the bandages which held the swaddling clothes in place. Holding the wriggling infant, she sponged it with the rose water that she had prepared for the occasion. Gently she anointed him with the acorn oil that Meg had fetched for her. She massaged the legs and arms and back. Then, in a clumsy fashion, she swaddled and bandaged him, gave him the sign of the cross, kissed him and put him to the breast and let him have his fill.

On the Sunday afternoon following the birth, Norma's father and mother came visiting.

Norma noticed the flickering, yet comprehensive, glance with which her father assessed the interior of the house before he greeted her in French.

"Je suis bien. Father" she replied, and appreciated the compliment in his smile. The French was their private concern, but English was the language in her house.

"My first grandchild," he said in English, turning to Meg.

She bobbed a token curtsy, "Yes Master, a strong lad."

Norma's mother walked straight to the cot and stood looking at the little face, lying with eyes closed, wanting to pick him up. The presence of Meg had an unconscious effect on the gathering. This was her kingdom, even if she remained in the background.

Benches were the usual seating in the house but Jacob

had made a straight backed chair where Norma could lean and rest. She was sitting in it when her parents arrived. She did not rise from the seat, leaving Meg to prepare the customary food and drink and take charge of the discussion.

Jacob, who had been outside, stooped through the doorway.

"Good day, Master Alleyn. Are ye well?"

"Aye Jacob. How does your way prosper?"

"The work goes forward now the weather improves. The calf crop bodes well for the settling time in the autumn."

"Now you are a father, you will need to make sure of your bargain," Alleyn pointed out.

"I think I will."

"The Auditors were not so sure, they thought that they had given you a hard bargain," laughed Alleyn. "I said naught at their council lest it went against you. I was upset in the way you took Norma, but I have seen enough of men to make me judge them by their actions, not their words."

"Thank thee Master." Jacob was pleased.

"You have now my grandson as well as my daughter. Guard them well. It is all I ask."

"There is a matter of moment, if it please you, Master," broke in Meg.

"And what is that?"

"Both Mistress Norma and the boy are well. But Twill be the custom, ere next Sabbath, to Christen the lad."

The Church and the Church's teaching had been an integral part of Norma's life since she was born, but the long winter had necessitated her absence from many of the services. Their holding was a good mile walk away on the more amenable farming land of the village. But Jacob had paid his respects regularly, and saved the fines for absence.

"Yes?" questioned Alleyn.

"Twould be a sore journey for the mistress, in her

condition, to travel uphill, the mile to Church. Tis a sufficient reason for the parson to travel by pony for a private baptism."

"You do ask for much," pointed out Norma's mother. "It is not a thing to be granted lightly."

"Nay," said Alleyn. "I shall arrange it. And Norma can present the boy at her Churching when she is strong enough."

And it was so. The afternoon passed in talk and planning and, before the week was out, Master William de Cherlton, the parson came and the baby was christened John. And his entry into paradise assured.

Meg had done her part and was ready to move on. She knew that there would be another birth next week and, probably, another after that. She pondered what was in store for this little one; growth and toil and rest and toil again. Her own life was immersed in a sea of births and deaths; corn sowing and harvests; ewe leaping and lambing; calves and piglets and chickens and the autumn killing for winter meat.

There was rumours in the countryside and tales aplenty of wars and battles. Would this lad be part of it?

It amused Norma to think that, contrary to the teaching of the parson, her mother had seemed to marry above her station, and that she herself, had taken a man in a lower standing than she had been brought up in. But then she was free, although her life was governed by the farm and the stock. Her mother had said that she had to help her husband in whatever he had to do. So she had taken note of the organisation of the manor house and her father's house, and had determined to do her best in the conditions which were part of her man's life.

After Meg went away Norma, with Peg, soon had the routine jobs organised. She enjoyed the early mornings and evenings with baby John and soon acquired the skill in moulding his limbs before she wrapped him up again. He was an energetic child and it worried her when he started a spell of crying and struggling in his mummified state. So she loosed his arms before the recognised time and he seemed to be satisfied.

Peg was a slim, bright, active eighteen year old, called Little because her mother was big, up the way, out the way, and in her domineering manner. Peg was not exactly slip-shod but, away from her mother, 'near enough' was 'good enough'. Norma enjoyed her company but by the end of a week she found that she was doing the jobs that Peg had left unfinished and, thanking her, said that she could manage by herself.

Norma enjoyed the day when they went to her Churching, seeing her friends and showing off her son. Father Jacob disappeared with his friends and did his own christening in the Old Lamb. It seemed a long walk back home and the chores to do before bedtime. But they were both young, and life was a time for living, even if the high lights had to be paid for in toil.

Norma's family was more or less split in two halves. There were only fourteen months between Alleyn and Pierre so that, as they grew up, they tended to act like twins. Their father Alleyn was well pleased with the tendency of the older boys to the academic way of life and even more pleased, in his shrewd assessment, that Roger showed a leaning towards the more practical life.

In many ways Norma was closer to her brother Roger than the two other two and was not surprised when, one wet Sunday afternoon, Roger rode a pony down to their holding. He made a great show of splashing through the puddles and bringing it to a sliding halt in the mud. Neither Jacob or Norma made any show of praise at his horsemanship.

Jacob doffed his bonnet and, in a broad peasant's voice said, "Welcome to ee, Master, to grace our 'umble abode."

Roger backed the pony to show it off. "What do you think of it?"

"Twould not avail much in a plew," quoth Jacob.

"It isn't a plough horse, you clod," laughed Roger as he slid off its back. "Where can I put it, out of the rain?"

"In there," said Norma pointing. "I'll go and make some mulled ale to take the discomfort out of the weather."

Norma was in a curious situation. She was well aware that, as was the custom, there would be a session of small talk before the real meaning of Roger's visit would be quietly introduced to the conversation. She was also aware that women were not supposed to have any opinions, or join in the real business discussions, but she had always been allowed to listen to the family talks. She had placed a pot of honey on the table and had opened a cupboard to take out a twist of paper.

"Ale broth," said Roger, "what has your friend in the kitchen let you have?"

"Ginger....but not much of it, and a clove."

She went to the warming ale and sprinkled some into it and added a measure of honey. While the men looked on she rough cut some bread and ladled the ale into two bowls. They paid her the compliment of sampling the brew before they relaxed to the talking.

Norma looked at the two men who meant so much in her life, the boy she grew up with and the man that she had given her life to. Roger with the accent of the Gentry and the enjoyment of the lifestyle of the peasants. Jacob with his ambition for the future but tending to hide it, burrowing unnoticed like a mole until the time came to surface. Both of them with their own problems.

Roger was wishing that it was a dry day so that he could have made an excuse and gone for a walk with Jacob to save her the embarrassment of being there when they had their say.

Jacob was in his element. He liked the dealer's ploys when they fenced for an opening, or playing cartes in the Lamb. To add spice to the occasion, he was not sure of the stakes, or the reason for Roger's visit on a stormy afternoon when he could have been comfortable at his own fireside.

A sudden squall drove the rain down from the Wrekin and battered on the house.

"We're in the dry," said Jacob. "Tis the recompense for foregoing my freedom." He waved his hand round the room.

Roger looked surprised, and then looked at Norma for her reaction.

"He means, when you and him used to spend the Sunday afternoons chasing the village maidens," she said.

"What know you of such things?"

"Only gossip," she laughed. "Only gossip."

"Oh," said Roger then, turning to Jacob. "Do you remember the last time we went out together?"

Jacob thought for a moment, trying to fathom the drift of the question. Was this why Roger was here, and what of it?

"We went to see the Knight at Tibberton return from his joustings," he ventured.

"Yes. Remember the palfrey that he won?"

"Aye. He let you ride it... You don't need a palfrey."

"No, but I had an offer of the pony I rode down just now. I had meant to show you it...if you had come up today."

Jacob knew, that Roger knew, that he had no intention of going to the manor that day. So where did the road lead to now? He looked at Norma to invite her into the riddle.

"I heard that the two of you came home from the Knight's feast and went straight to work next morning," she said. "Without bed. In the village at least."

"Only gossip," Roger held up his hands. "Only gossip."

"Mother does not gossip," she suggested.

"Twas a good night," said Jacob. "We heard that Sir Richard had the best tournaments in years and the celebration went on for days. We but helped to congratulate him."

"My father thinks that I should marry and settle on the land that is our due from the manor," said Roger unexpectedly. "And stay at home more often, of course."

That took them by surprise. But not Jacob. The reason for the visit began to be clearer and he was not sure whether he liked it or not.

"We have been comrades for many years," he said, "tis only because ye have not a companion to abet you in your free time...thinking like that, I mean. I only wed to be able to claim the land."

Norma jumped up and refilled the bowls. "Drink your broth and let it clear your brains." She looked at Jacob. "That may have been said in jest, but it is cruel to both Roger and I. It is true that you and I are freemen, and Roger is tied to the manor. But we are all alike, tied to this land for a living. It is not a thing to mention among friends."

They were all quiet while they supped the broth.

"What is on y'r mind?" asked Jacob, to get the conversation going again.

"It is true that marriage was mentioned, but not who to."

"There is one at Longford, but she is too proud to have you," said Norma.

"You will be hard put to find one like Norma," said Jacob.

"There is one at Tibberton," ventured Roger.

'This is it,' thought Jacob, and kept thinking hard.

"Who?" he asked, as innocently as he could.

"The daughter of the knight... At least she is accepted as his daughter. Her mother is his housekeeper, but her man went missing years ago and cannot be found to divorce him, and let them be wed."

"What is she like?" asked Norma.

"What do you think, Jacob?" Roger asked him.

Well, what did he think?.

"She's a bit older than me," he answered. "Well about your age Roger. A well favoured lass."

"That's not what I meant," objected Norma.

Jacob knew that was not what she meant.

"She did land work on the demesne at Caynton," he said. "And then worked in the Caynton Manor house, because there was not enough work at Tibberton. Her father was a good worker, better than most. But it was a sin to leave the family to the care of the knight. Her mother and her brothers are well respected."

What more could he say? She might have been sitting where Norma was sitting now!

"What will father say?" asked Norma.

"By the way, have you asked her yet?" asked Jacob

Roger's face lit up with the old devilry that Jacob knew so well, and had matched on many an occasion.

"No," he said. "But...."

Jacob nodded. He had a good idea of what the outcome would be.

CHAPTER ELEVEN

Although he was not aware of it, young John, son of Jacob o' the Marsh, had no way of knowing that he was the next generation of the family that his grandfather had accepted, the family that his mother had planned, and a father who had determined that he was to have a very different upbringing.

He learned many lessons in a haphazard sort of way, but he had the instruction of both his father and his mother to guide him. His ears were the first receptors of the world around him. The person who was always there, and fed him, made a lot of noises. Another one, who was only there sometimes was quiet, but used to lift him off the bed and swing him round. He felt safe and liked it. Lying in his cot and listening to the sounds, he could hear, far away, a chorus of deep baas and plaintive bleatings. A sound that would be with him until he could hear no more.

Sometimes he would be wrapped up and taken outside and laid down where it felt warm and his mother would bend down and work and talk to him at the same time. All around him were different noises coming from all directions, some below him, some above, some very faint.

He tried to hear the noises that she said. He tried to hold his head high and look around him. He saw the tall shapes of different colours and the other shapes above his head making shrill noises. The round little shapes at his mother's feet made short noises as they moved quickly about.

He went with his father and mother one day with some some strange animals. He was left lying near a tall plant where he cold see them. They went off and his mother made loud noises and prodded the animals, while his father followed behind them with a thing which stuck in the ground. After a while they sat down and his father ate something and he had a feed from his mother.

He found, in time, that he could stand and walk like his father did when he went away. He was to learn, as he grew older and could see further, the water with the rushes and wild fowl and stunted trees in the valley which was to be his home for years to come.

John found that his mother said 'No' when he wanted to walk to some places, but he took no notice and kept going until she came and carried him back. He found that the round things moving on the ground made clucking noises and scratched with their feet and bobbed up and down and pecked at the ground. If he moved up to them fast they flopped away and called out loud. He liked that and did it often until his mother made him stop.

One day one of the round things came out of some long plants, making a loud noise. He went in to see what was there but the long stuff burned his hand and face. He found some smooth white stones. When he banged two of them together they broke and yellow stuff went all over his hand and his smock. When his mother found him she laughed and told him not to do it again. He heard her tell his father about hens and eggs and nettles. They both laughed at that.

When he found more of the stones he was careful and took them in to his mother who said 'Go.o.od'. That pleased him.

He soon learned the noises which meant something. His mother was always telling him things but the words were strange to him. He soon learned 'quiet' and 'come here' and ' keep still', although he pretended that he was not sure what she meant. His mother was always moving about but, at times she would stop and show him something. He pretended to listen but would rather have done it his own way.

His first winter was cold and went on for a long time. Sometimes, when he looked outside the house, he couldn't see very far and his mother said that it was raining and that he had better bide indoors. But he went out when she went to do her chores and he liked the splash of the water on his face. His mother was angry and took all his clothes off and rubbed him hard with a cloth, saying that he would get the ague.

It surprised him when the water went hard. Sometimes, when he looked out, the whole place was covered in white and it hurt his eyes to look at it. That was when the white came down like feathers but when he tried to catch them they floated away. His mother called it snow and he had to stay indoors.

At Christmas Jacob and Norma had carried him up to the manor. It was the first time that he had been through the snow to where there was a lot of people and there was laughing and singing. When he felt tired he was put into a corner to fall asleep.

His mother was tall and dark among the other women. She held him by the hand when a tall man with black hair and eyes looked at him sternly and asked his mother something.

She said," Yes."

He felt the man's hand on his head as he said," Bon." And then the man kissed his mother on both cheeks and she bobbed down and bent her head.

"My father." She told him, as if that were enough.

Jacob was proud of his son. To John he was big and his clothes smelled queer and exciting. He was a quiet man with kind eyes but they could blaze hard when Jacob spoke sharply to him about something which he ought not to do. He stopped doing it again.... if he was likely to be caught.

His father showed him some 'oxen' one day. They were

very big but John didn't feel frightened. They were the ones that his mother had prodded with the stick. His father put him on the back of one and he held on tight to the rough coat. His father looked pleased.

When he grew bigger his mother put a tray, with sand in it, on the floor and give him a stick to make marks on it.

"Now then you have to learn," she told him. She had been brought up in a writing family and was determined to do the best for him.

She showed him some marks on paper and called them letters. He tried to make them in the sand and join them together to make a word like 'oxen', 'sheep', 'hens' and 'trees'. He was soon bored with it.

There were some times he enjoyed it, when he could read the words. These were good days, especially if his mother had made some batch cakes when she was baking the bread. If he had done well she would butter one and let him have it.

She was always getting at him, even when he was outside; 'Do this right', 'Do that this way'. He got fed up being told what to do and did it her way for a bit of peace. He found that it was usually a better way. That taught him a lesson.

Sometimes the not-so-big people would come down the hill and run about through the bushes where there were no oxen. He could hear them splashing in the brook and calling to each other. When they came back, his mother gave them some ale with water in it . They were very quiet when she looked at them and, when they had finished, they said,

"Thank thee kindly, Mistress Jacob." and then they ran off laughing and yelling. He wanted to go with them but his legs were too short for running fast. His mother said that they came from Adeney.

Once, in the long days when the sun was shining all day, his father and mother took him up to where some people were, and there was much fun and feasting. His mother said. "You are a big boy now but guard yourself from mischief." And sent him off amongst the others. There were some boys of his own size and he played with them. They wrestled and ran about and pretended to fight.

They watched the dancers with coloured streamers round the big pole and men who clashed sticks and had bells on their legs. There was a man with a beast that did a silly dance. The animal was as big as an ox and was on a chain. He watched his father shooting his bow and he seemed to get something because they all said that he was the best. There were some silly girls there who ran away when they teased them.

And there was plenty to eat.

When it came dark, somebody lit a big fire and everybody danced round it. Later he and his friends fell asleep while the big people kept drinking and dancing and the men kept wrestling with the young women.

One day an old lady who was kind to him, came to the house and they sent him out to play. When they let him back into the house his mother had a little baby all wrapped up. He had seen where ox calves and lambs came from but he wondered where the baby came from.

The old lady had put her arm on his shoulder to take him to his mother who was lying in bed. He had never seen his mother in bed before in the day time and it looked strange.

"John, here is thy little brother. Ye will have some company now I warrant ye."

They named the baby, Dickon. It was too small to play with and his mother spent most of the time with it. So he went outside and continued to play on his own.

His mother was busier than ever with the baby, but she kept telling him sayings and proverbs and making him learn them; 'Do as you would be done by'; 'Do not be greedy at the table': 'Watch people who have a axe to grind'. She taught him to count with his fingers, and made him measure by taking steps, and counting the geese as they moved about. All these skills he would need when he would have to work his land and cattle and have money to reckon.

One day Jacob took him to the hay field. He had taken him there before and would carry him home on his shoulders but this time he said.

"You be too big to carry now."

And so John had to walk.

Some other men who came to help with the hay laughed with him.

"John, son of Jacob, thou dost grow apace."

They put their hands on his head to measure his height against the belts on their smocks.

"Thou wilt soon be big enough to help thy father."

By the time he knew that he was four years old he had seen the rain and the snow and the falling leaves which he chased and sometimes caught before they reached the ground; he knew that the grass grew and died and came again; that short days grew longer and warmer and then the snow came again when the days grew short.

He learned that, all too soon, the days of all play were over.

John noticed that he was too big for a lot of things since he had a baby brother. Now that his mother was busy, it became his task to feed the hens and the pigs and collect the eggs. His father told him that he had been able to milk at his age, so his mother showed him how it was done. He was too small to carry the milk so he tried to churn the milk for butter, but he found that he was not strong enough to keep the Dolly going up and down. His mother would say 'Good Boy' and finish the churning.

Jacob always had plenty work to do, but was ever ready to tutor his son. When he was near, he would keep showing him different things. John had difficulty in remembering them all, although he tried. His father found him a little axe and kept it sharp for him and every day he had to chop some of the smaller sticks when he fetched the peat turves for the fire.

Jacob, remembering Will Turner's bow, had the bower at the manor make a small one. He told John that now he was a little man of five he could have a real bow, a stretcher to protect his arm and arrows to match. He told him that the bow was made of yew wood and that he would teach him to use it properly. John was annoyed that his lack of strength did not allow him to draw it to full stretch, but his father only laughed and said that it would come in time. So he spent hours practising and handling it the way his father had been taught. But it was a real bow and it took some time.

John found, that if he sat down for a rest and kept quiet, he could see all sorts of birds as they flew among the trees, and bright coloured flies in the bushes. He noticed the bees, which came from the two straw beeskeps near the house, coming and visiting the flowers and then going back again. He tried to follow them and noticed that they all took the same path through the air.

He found some ants one day and poked a stick down the hole to see them run about. He didn't notice them getting on his legs until they began to bite him. That taught him a lesson.

He had seen how his father emptied the eel basket in the creek and, on one of his journeys, he tried to haul it out of the water. In his efforts with the heavy creel he fell in. Fortunately he was tall enough to get his head out of the water when he stood up. That taught him another lesson.

He was beginning to explore further afield, trying to find the world that his mother had been telling him about. One day he crossed the valley to see the small river which meandered through the woods where the rough trees grew.

In the spring the whole valley was covered with a mass of yellow marigolds, willow catkins and a smother of hawthorn blossom. Ducks and swans, with outspread wings, landing on the waters with the spray flying; waterhens skimming the water on their red legs.

He had learned that the voice of the cuckoo brought the swooping arrow tailed swallows, and the flitting shapes of the bats in the dusk of evening. Corncrakes croaking all night.

He had done his childish best to scare the marauders off his father's corn and had eaten some of the rook fledglings who had fallen to his father's bow.

He had heard the ghostly skeins of geese at the time of the falling leaves. And spent the long evenings sitting by the fire, rough scraping some wood for his father to carve into a wooden spoon or a beech trencher.

Jacob had never lost the secretive nature which his early upbringing had forced upon him and, although there was a tacit understanding between Norma and himself, he found it difficult to openly discuss his feelings with her. Nevertheless the time that he had spent with the widow had opened his eyes to many things, and he found that he was seeing the mistakes in his youth in the light of his relationship with both John and Norma.

"Think thee, Mistress," he asked her, one evening when the good weather had given them an idle moment in the setting sun. "Think thee that we make his life too easy?"

Norma looked at him with surprise, not at what he had said, but the fact that he had said it. Jacob was looking to where John and Dickon. were romping together further down the hill.

"In what way?" she asked cautiously.

"When I was his age, I was a man... albeit a little one at that." He laughed.

"You have never said anything before this, of your boyhood. Was it hard?"

"I didn't know any better then. At the time I thought that it was....as it had to be. But I liked it not." He was quiet for a while, thinking back to the early days. "Maybe my mother felt the same." He sounded surprised as if he had never thought of that before.

"Has it done you any harm?" she asked.

"Mebbe yes, maybe no." He sounded as if he wasn't sure, and wanted somebody to inform him.

This was a new Jacob to Norma. The tough, unlettered, strong, wilful boy who had seemed to know his own mind, and had unconsciously dominated her life from as far back as she could remember. She thought of her father and her brothers, seemingly confident in their own way of life. Did they also question their own motives?

"Our lives are changing," she said, "...as we make them change. For good or ill, who knows?"

"I always wanted some land, so that I should be free in truth. Now we have it, we still toil like peasants. Save that we enjoy the increase...if God doth give us any, as my mother used to say."

"My father had land and a good living, almost like the Gentry," she said. "...but was tied to the manor. I only married you to have the standing of a free woman. And now I have the life of a bondwoman." Norma's laugh had the teasing enjoyment of a girl.

Jacob riled up with a strong oath on his tongue, until he saw the mischief in her eyes.

"God's a mercy, woman," he gasped. "Never tempt me like that again. A woman once told me that I was a tempestuous man, but that I would find a woman who was waiting for me. And that I should treat her well."

He glared at her, both conscious that they had touched a hidden spot that had been tacitly ignored between them, since Norma had rebuked him long a go. She glanced away to where the boys were engrossed in their own play and, when he pulled her roughly to her feet, she went willingly with him.

The almost business-like handfast, the taking and giving of strength and comfort in the stresses of toil and setbacks, were superseded and purged in the acceptance by a man of his woman, and a woman of her man.

Norma had been teaching John to count for people's ages and had told him that he was seven years old.

"You are now a young man and will be treated by everyone as a grown up with your responsibilities, and punishment if you do err," she told him.

One day he heard his father and mother talking to each other." It's time the boy attended the school," his mother said.

"Why should he?" asked his father.

"It's for his own good. We are fortunate to have a parson to teach a school on the manor. There is plenty of land to assart near us, and he will need his counting and reading to ...."

"...to be like your brothers? And go to the school in Newborough?" Jacob broke in.

"Nay. If they have land, like my father, they will need a man to farm it. It will be better for John to farm his own land and know the art of his own buying and selling," she argued.

"But he is of an age to work now. He does his tasks well.

And we need him." he objected.

"Let him go there until noon. He can do his chores before he goes and his other work in the afternoon," she pointed out.

"Tis a long way to walk, each morning," his father put in as an excuse.

She brushed it aside. "His legs are strong enough and will grow to the task."

"You are a managing woman, Mistress Norma. But you do y'r share of work. I warrant you," laughed Jacob, giving in.

John felt his father looking at him. "Would ye like that John?" asked his father.

John thought of the companionship of the other boys and said, "I would like that."

"Tis settled then. We will have words with the Cleric on Sunday," decided his father.

John had gone, as usual, to the Church with his parents on Sunday.

"It is incumbent on the Church to educate bright lads for the benefit of the Church," said the Parson when he was approached by John's parents.

"Nay," said Jacob. "If it please God, he will farm the land we will have when it is beyond me."

"It is the English he needs," said his mother. "As you well know... begging your pardon, sir." She felt surprised at her show of determination against authority.

The parson permitted a smile of approbation to soften his eyes. "You have much of your father in you mistress Norma. But one does not argue with the Church, my daughter. Have you still the French tongue?"

"And John also...for some things." she admitted.

"It is a strange world today. Many changes." He turned

to John. “How many summers have you boy ?”

“My mother doth count seven, Master.”

“It is well.” He turned to Norma. “It is the age to profit for the breaking of every child to goodness or lewdness.” Turning to John. “Have you a taste for learning ?”

John brought up to be a man, had a sudden feeling of his smallness.

“I know not, sir, but my mother hath been instructing me.”

“As well she might. There is much happening in the world beyond our village. It will be the man who knows both the land and his books who will survive. You know not, I warrant, the rod? Tis on thine own head to vouchsafe its acquaintance.”

John began to think that there might be some hidden snags in this school venture. He was looking forward to the company and, in a way, the extra learning building on the start that he had from his mother. But, growing up on his own had given him an independence which he had cherished and was determined to retain.

“Tis a long journey in the morning. When does school begin?” asked his father.

“The first bell is seven of the clock in the morning, sharp. They tarry there until eleven of the clock. Returning at two of the clock in the afternoon.”

“There is work that is his on the farm,” explained Norma. “Is it permitted that he comes only in the morning?”

“It is not usual,” objected the priest.

“I can supervise at home,” she offered.

“There will be times when he will be needed...at harvest and other times,” broke in Jacob.

“We must consider it when the time arrives,” was the only allowance that the parson would make.

A week later John set off with his script containing bread and cheese and a leathern bottle of ale. The excitement of a new adventure seemed to shorten the journey there, and the welcome of his known friends made it worth while. The constriction of the four walls was balanced by the freedom of the walk home.

CHAPTER TWELVE

John had been looking forward to going to school, as a step away from the restrictions of his home life, the constant work that he had to do, and the wet moors of his flat valley. He had never felt lonely when he was growing up on his own but he had enjoyed being with the other boys when he went up to the manor and church. When he arrived there he found that the brief friendship he had known was different from the day-to-day contact which showed up the lazy-bones, the cheats, the bullies. He began to learn how to balance his own personality against the demands of the others, when to be selfish and when to give way.

There were only ten pupils of different ages. Some of them were girls. He did not know much about girls, but some of the other boys did.

Walt, son of Colley the Brewer, was the oldest and was already taking time off for his adult work load. He was the bell-wether of the flock but his ready laugh softened his rude dominance.

Mutchkin, the blacksmith's son, was a tall thin lad. He had a pleasant, self-effacing manner and always had a ready excuse for his usually unfinished work. His constant association with the bundle of birch twigs made little difference to his lack of ambition. John could never reconcile Mutchkin's attitude with the proverbs which, he had understood from his mother, were obligatory for a successful life.

From the alphabet, which he had learned from his mother, the instruction proceeded to the Psalter, learning the

Psalms one by one, copying them on to slates, and finally repeating them off by heart.

He learned that the schoolmaster had to be treated with great respect, indeed feared. Any slight misdemeanour resulted in physical punishment, which, it seemed, was part of the Church's teaching of morals. This was carried out with the bundle of birch twigs applied to the back or buttocks. John soon found that he was not immune from its acquaintance. What he could not understand was that getting it seemed to be an entry into the companionship of the other boys.

From his mother he had learned the PaterNoster by heart and heard some of the Bible stories and now he was daily being exhorted to profit by diligence and obedience.

Alison Reeves was a pale girl, the youngest of the reeve's children. She was two years older than John and almost ready to leave school. Her main reason for attending school was to be a help to her father in providing an account of his duties on the estate. She had suffered some fever in her younger days which had left her physically weaker than her peers. She might have been despised by her brothers if it had not been for her efforts to take an equal share in their lives.

Her thinness gave her an excuse for not joining in the rougher games but there was a kindliness about her manner. She was tall for her age, but so was John, so they were on eye-level with each other. Her quiet assured manner and tidy appearance appealed to him and in the classroom they often sat together and he was astute enough to take the help that she gave him without any condescension from him to her girl-hood status.

John never got used to the inactivity of sitting still and was always ready for the eleven o'clock break to rest his behind. When he had the time to play in the outside games he found the rumbustious excercise to his liking. Some of the older girls joined in at times.

Madge, Walt's sister, was a burly girl but very agile. One day when they were playing follow-my-leader she slipped. As she fell and rolled over, her skirt rode up over her legs.

"Madge hath upended herself," the boys yelled as she kicked her legs in the air.

It was the first time John had seen a girl's legs and he looked amazed as she lay laughing with her legs splayed out.

For a moment he thought that she was injured, the absence of anything at the foot of her belly except a pink slit. Then, as the realisation dawned on him he felt himself go red as he turned away, with the laughter of the others in his ears.

But he was a big boy, and quick with it, and had the fists to prove it. So that, when they all came together again, John's discomfiture was overlooked.

Jacob was well aware of the similarity of his home to that of the poorer serf's dwellings. A lean-to on the outside was now used as a brew and bake house where Norma extemporised the cooking arrangements and butter and cheese making. But he was bedevilled by the lack of money and had to wait for the long term return from the slow maturing oxen stock.

His estimate of the work with the cattle herd in respect to the return was not quite as he thought it would be. Most of the neat cows were on loan to the villagers and the calves, which they needed each year to keep the cows in milk, were the property of the manor. His share of every fifth calf was a long time in maturing. It took him some time to organise the work to his own best advantage. Thinking of the future and how to build up his own herd John claimed most of his allowance in heifer calves. As the bailiff and the reeve were more interested in draught animals and meat they raised no objection with the Auditors.

Although there were plenty of stunted trees which he could cut for fire-bote in the wet valley bottom he had used his allowance of Scot wood and had marked some well grown oaks with the bend suitable for making two gable crucks. It took him two winters to get the time to fell the trees and trail them home and weather them, using the work to break in the young oxen to draught work.

Young John was excited by the idea of a new house and, one day on the way home from school, he met Walt outside the Inn and went in to have a look at a real house.

The Inn, built over a cellar, was a long two storied building of a drinking room, brewhouse, and malting house joined together under one roof. When he went in through the Inn door with Walt he felt the tingle of the atmosphere; the malty smell, and the warmth and heady aroma of sin. In the dim light he could see the trestles and benches and, at the brewhouse end, a fireplace that looked, to him, big enough to burn a tree. It seemed, to him, a wonderful arrangement compared to his mother's weekly home brewing set up.

Walt's mother, black as a rook and bowed with years of fetching jugs up the stairs from from the cellar, laughed at him with her bright witch's eyes.

"Good day, young master. Thy pleasure on this thy visit.?"

Jonathon, the old Ridingman, leaning on his stick in the inglenook cackled. "A pewter tankard for the gentry Mistress Mabel."

She splashed some ale out of a large jug and handed it to John.

"Thy good health, young master."

John, used to the mild brew of his mother and excited by the welcome, took a fair swig at the pot before he noticed the different taste as the strong brew swam around in his belly. He put the half empty tankard down.

"What bringeth thee here young master.?"

"My father plans to build a house. I wish to see yours."

The wall opposite the brewhouse end had a door and he followed Walt through it into a smaller room with a low sleeping loft reached by a ladder.

"The girls room up there," said Walt. "When we were youngsters we all slept there. Twas fun then in the dark, if we kept quiet. Madge will tell thee." He laughed.

John thought not. He could cope with Walt any day but, thinking on the parson's words, he could see the fires of hell in Madge's brilliant dark brown eyes.

The way up to the village was only a wide path meandering through the trees. It was wide because, now and again, it was used by an ox-wagon in the charge of men dressed in long woollen cloaks. He learned that they were monks and they farmed the Adeney estate for an Abbey. Sometimes they would drive sheep along the road, but mostly they had garden produce on the wagons. His mother told him that they sold the goods in Newborough market. When he met them he did his reverence, as he had been taught, in answer to their "Good morrow, my son" spoken in soft, kindly voices.

He did not understand, at the time, why the land that his father used was smothered in trees and lower than the land used by the Monks. And the stock that they had were sheep rather than the oxen which his father had. When he spoke about it to his father, he was surprised to hear the antagonism in Jacob's voice. It seemed that the monks were shepherds. This placed them, in his mind, on a lower level than the ox-men.

The journey, after lessons, gave John an opportunity to take different paths on his way home and learn, first hand, of the occupations on the manor. He was welcomed by some of the old men and often stopped to talk to them.

Thom the shepherd was old. At least his head hair was white under his conical bonnet, and the fuzz of hair on his throat and under his chin. His face was clean shaven and as brown as a nut. John's mother said that was because the only time that he washed it was when he had a shave on Saturday to be ready for the church service on Sunday. His eyes were a pale grayey blue which could be as hard as ice when he was displeased and yet soft as a woman's when his sheep ailed or he had a difficult lambing.

He was not a tall man but his back was straight, not bowed with the constant toil in the fields. He took to John because John's father was a herdsman.

"That be the way you have it so," he told him. But he didn't like the oxen. "Big brainless buggers." He called them. "They do need a good sharp prick on the arse to even make them move. Mind you they have their uses, with their great greedy tongues tearing at the rough grass and gulping it down. Now look at the sheep which do nibble daintily at the young short stuff."

"We need them both," said John.

"Aye, I suppose so. They be both God's creatures. Do you notice how they always kneel before they lie down, and kneel again on their front legs before they arise?.....Do ye say your prayers night and morning, John?"

"Aye Master Thom. And PaterNosters."

"Another thing Master John. Remember y'r Scriptures. The Good Shepherd was not an hireling. Look after y'r animals as if they were y'r own."

But John knew that story, and that Thom's sheep were not his own. But his father's oxen were his own. A germ of an idea, sown by chance, which was to lie dormant. That's how the winter wheat grows. A month in the cold hard ground to root, and then the sprouts come alive. And the seed that was sown that day was to bring forth its harvest in due course.

As John grew older and his legs grew stronger his world seemed to grow smaller as he could move from place to place in a shorter time. His home, the pivot of his world, was a place to visit and sleep in. His mother's influence was still strong but was only a small part of the learning process which was developing him.

He instinctively appreciated that the effect of the school was for his good. While he improved in reading, a thing his father could not do, he had no great belief in the stories, used in the school, as examples. But he realised the capabilities of his mother in business matters and how much of a help that Alison must be to her father.

The reeve could make his counting marks and knew every operation of the farm work by memory but, when the auditors made their yearly accounts, he had to rely on someone else to write them down.

Alison had now left school and, although he missed her, John did not see her very often.

The next summer was long and dry and Jacob was kept busy, both on his own land and on the demesne. True to his own upbringing, but remembering his years of working on his own, he found John plenty to do in his afternoons after school, both on the arable work on his own land and on demesne work; pricking the oxen at the fallow ploughing times; raking hay at hay harvest; weeding corn in August; gathering the corn at corn harvest. The bird scaring was the task of the younger children and he kept him from that.

John's brother, Dickon, followed him to school in due course. Dickon, slimmer built than John and darker of visage, had more of his mother's family in him. When he was a youngster John resented his quietness but could not find fault with the way he took his share of the household work and on jobs the farm. Like most growing lads, they both despised and admired their father and, as the years passed, used him as their lodestone, example, and the champion to be dethroned.

Dickon had fallen heir to John's first bow. He was more conscientious in his practise than John, with a natural quickness of hand and eye. In the usual run of things John's superior age and weight gave him the advantage at work and in their play fighting. But Dickon had the edge when precision was called for. His dark good looks made him the favourite with the girls, and their mothers as well.

Norma, trying not to show favourites, was equally hard on both of them, although with his cunning, Dickon always came out best. His aptitude for French pleased her but he was no better than John in his schoolwork.

As they grew older it was John who took the plough while Dickon had the lowly part of pricking the oxen.

They ran into trouble one morning when they were hunting in the marsh for plover's nests. They heard a loud bellowing and crashing in the scrub bushes and went to investigate. A heifer had calved before her time and was at a loss with this strange body flopping round her feet and nosing at her belly. She was hooking the calf away from her and tossing it around.

John had his staff but Dickon, in his impetuous way, jumped into the fray, trying to pull the calf to safety. A vicious sweep of the horns from the maddened beast caught his smock and slung him into a nearby bush. John yelled and swung his staff cracking the heifer on the horns. Momentarily surprised, the heifer backed off letting John check that the calf was still alive.

Jacob, who had heard the tumult, appeared on the scene at a run and, with John's help quietened the heifer, and let her taste her calf. John turned to rescue Dickon from the bush. He was badly bruised but nothing broken.

"Tis lucky you are," said Jacob. "Never attempt anything like that again. Come for me first. You're more important than any bloody calf."

Gently he cradled Dickon in his arms and trudged off home.

Fortunately a torn smock and bad bruises was the total damage and Dickon lived to learn his lesson. As did John, who was not very pleased at the way his father had shown a favouritism to Dickon.

Although their days were often filled with drudgery to suit the seasons there were days fixed by the Church as Holy Days when, after the morning service, the villagers gathered together to enjoy some merriment. One of the days, not associated with the Church, came after the frost and snow of January and February and the wet west winds blowing from the Wrekin in April.

It was the May Day.

It seemed as if the world was coming to life again. They had heard the rooks in their March courting, cawing and chattering in the tall trees, and seen the fledglings trying their wings. John was awakened most mornings by the before dawn bird chorus. The blackthorn blossom studded the copse edges and the moors with a blaze of mock snow drifts. Down in the Wildmoors the brilliant slashes of marigolds shone at the feet of the grey-green willows. The country had survived the chill of the Blackthorn blossom winter.

John knew the days and the months and had noticed his

mother's tallies to show that it was the first day of May. At home, on the day, they were up early to get the stock work finished by dawn and then set off to the manor to join the other villagers who had been out gathering the spring flowers and hauling in the tree, which had been felled in the forest, for the Maypole dancing. The maypole was to be set up opposite The Old Lamb Inn where the road from the valley made a three cornered village green with the main road through the village.

On some long trestle tables, food from the Manor House and other donors, was spread out. A joint of saltmeat kept specially for the day, long soaked and boiled and left to cool; a 'christening chine' from the blacksmith's specially fed pig, with two inches of fat as soft as butter (the blacksmith's wife was beyond having any more christenings); dried apple pastries; wheaten loaves baked in the Manor House ovens; baked eggs from the new seasons crop from the poultry; pork sausages with whiskers, spare from a cottager with no family; some fish pies.

In the pin-fold, next to the green, a fire had been lit before dawn by the blacksmith's apprentice and his mates and a barren ewe, skinned and dressed was slowly being turned to provide a cut of mutton for the feast. The younger ones, free from restraint, began their day early, running and chasing, dodging between the adults.

With much ordering and counter-ordering the stay ropes and streamers were attached to the Maypole and, amid shouts and cheers the oxen laid on their yokes and pulled the long tree skywards. A deal of banging on the pins readied the tree for the dancing later on.

Two fiddlers and a drummer had been hired from Newborough for the Maypole music and the green dancing to end the day and had brought some Morris dancers to team up with those from the village. They were busy in the Inn, tuning their fiddles and winding themselves up with Colley's choice brew. Outside the Inn was a barrel of penny ale for the women and children.

The women busied themselves with the mayflower marigolds, tying them in bunches head down on the house doors and any likely spot around the green. So bright against the dark background they seemed like daylight lamps in a fairy circle.

The festivities began with the children's sports in order to run the excess excitement out of them. As the age of twelve was the dividing line it led to many inequalities. But by devious means they all enjoyed the excitement of getting something, except the winner, who had the admitted honour of being cock-of-the-walk. At least until the next year when he or she would possibly be competing with the young adults and would then be last in the line.

John was too heavy legged in the foot races but in the wrestling it looked as if he was going to be King until he met Mutchkin. He smiled confidently to himself as they took hold. And then he found that he had a bundle of string in his hands as Mutchkin gave and twisted until, with a sudden feint, he swung John down, flat on his back. John was disappointed and mad with himself. But, as with other events in his life, he remembered one of the sayings of his mother. 'It is the tree that yields to the wind that stands the storm.'

It seemed to be appropriate that Mutchkin, in his twelfth year, should be King of one of the sports as he had been paired with Madge who was Queen of the May.

The men had built a bower and a throne for Madge where she sat resplendent in a new gown. She fairly enjoyed the adulation but appeared envious when the young women's races were taking place.

He kept watching Alison, thin and wiry, racing against the other young women but she did not do very well although she danced the Maypole gracefully.

The highlight, for John, was the men's wrestling. He yelled as Walt downed one man after another until he met the Blacksmith. Maykin just planted his feet and stood his ground and let Walt strain and tug, Then he seemed to straighten himself and, without effort, lifted Walt off his feet and slammed him down on his back. The cheers were still ringing when he reached down, grabbed Walt's tunic and, with one hand, lifted him to his feet, let out a laugh which rumbled deep in his chest, and patted Walt on the back. After all, three stone of weight is a lot of handicap to a lad of fourteen.

Jacob had brought Will Turner's bow which he had lovingly cherished through the years. They had a short target to one side of the festivities and although the competition was keen he managed to preserve the reputation that he had acquired. As Norma said to him afterwards, "Will Turner would have been pleased."

After the ewe had been stripped to the bone and dismembered, the fire was piled up to lighten the scene for the evening dancing.

John met Alison a few times throughout the long and exciting day. They would exchange a few words and then drift apart. He felt that he was too old for the younger children and she looked too young beside the other single women.

As dusk descended, the fire made a pool of light for the dancing with the onlookers sitting in a darkened circle. Some of the women had gone home with the younger children but there were enough left to make the evening go with a swing.

The fiddlers and the drummer were seated by this time, playing their instruments by instinct as they had constant 'wets' from the tankards between their feet. The penny ale in the barrel had run dry and John and the others had graduated to the better brew from inside the Inn. As he joined the cavorting couples John felt the music reaching inside him right down to his toes. The older men seemed to be neglecting Alison. She was the reeve's daughter and, of course, not to be trifled with. John danced with her once. And then again. She looked as if she enjoyed it although it was warm work and, between them, they emptied John's flagon.

He noticed some of the couples disappearing into the darkness. Feeling partly daring, partly inquisitive, partly frightened he gently led her, willingly, out of the light. In the darkness she walked close to him so that he put his arm around her when she stumbled. She stopped and he turned her to him. They were both of the same height. He kissed her. And then he kissed her again. Instinctively he lowered her to the ground. He could feel her small hard breasts through her sweat damp smock as his hands roamed to her skirts.

She lay motionless while he fondled her and then, reluctantly, she pushed her skirts down and stood up. He tried to follow her.

"Nay, that is enough," she said. "Tis better we return to the fire. Ye must take that way. I will take this path. If ye say a thing about this doing, then I will blame ye and thou wilt be in trouble."

He watched her go, silhouetted against the fire light glow.

In a year or two, he reckoned, he would be a grown man. It seemed to him that he was learning a mort of lessons ready for that day.

CHAPTER THIRTEEN

Atherton, the gamekeeper, had grown to be a tall thin man, a dweller in the woods, living alone. After his mother died he shared the house, and the gamekeeping, with his father until the arthritis had taken taken its toll on the older man and left him on his own. It was said that his grandfather had been a falconer in the years when the King's Laws ruled the forests and the taking of game. That was in the days when a mewed sparrowhawk was the yearly token rent for the manor. The custom had fallen into disuse, but Atherton knew all the eyries of the kestrels and sparrowhawks and the heronries, the pheasants nests as well.

Sometimes, when Atherton came down to inspect the fishing and the woodlands in the valley bottom, John would have a talk with him. Of course, his father had warned him about the power of the gamekeeper without, as it so happened, allowing him to know the close hidden relationship that they both enjoyed. So he was very respectful to him, as a youngster should be to one in authority.

John knew that his father had been netting the fish in the meres for the manor house. Although all the fish that Jacob caught did not arrive at the intended destination, Atherton spoke well of the task that Jacob carried out for him, and also the netting of the conies in the bottom warren. He didn't seem to know that some of the conies never left the farm, either. John thought it was better not to tell him.

Atherton instructed him that if he ever saw or heard the vandals from Newborough poaching in the valley he would be obliged if John would let him know. He also implied that the wrath of an irate God would fall on anybody interfering with the pheasants, either in the nest or roosting in the trees. John could not understand why such a simple man could be in such a responsible position on the manor. When he said so to his father, he was surprised at the knowing look in his father's eyes.

"Aye," said Jacob, "a simple man." And then walked off laughing to himself.

When he arrived home one day he found that the midwife was there and that he had a baby sister. He knew a thing or two about girls and babies by that time and was not quite sure whether he was pleased or not about the baby.

He found that the house was suddenly too small for everybody. He and Dickon and his father fetched their palliasses from the store and spread them in a corner of the room. The midwife said that she was fine, thank you, and slept in the chair.

In the morning they were pleased to escape from the thick fug of the room into the biting cold dark, and the freshness of the pre-dawn air. When they had finished their yard chores they found that the beds had been stacked away, making room for a trestle-table with ale and bread and cheese to fortify them for the coming day.

Norma, still retaining the pride in her French descent called the baby Avril, after her birth month. Avril never went to school, but Norma took great pains in making sure that she had all the knowledge that she would require.

One afternoon John was working on the farm for his father when, a very fine gentleman rode down to the farm with a servant riding on a pony behind him.

"Boy. I seek Jacob the herdsman," he said in a very stern voice.

John, who had been well tutored in showing respect for

his betters, answered, "He is with the oxen down by the marsh, if it please thee, my Lord."

"And where may that be?"

"That be the path, Master."

Without a word, the gentleman wheeled his horse, the pony following.

Some time later John saw them ride up the hill, talking together and taking a great interest in all that they could see.

At supper that night, Jacob said, "I have been requested to deliver ten oxen at Church Aston."

"Take them? And who will pay?" asked Norma.

"I like it not. The gentleman has made a bargain with the bailiff."

"But the bailiff has been elsewhere these last two weeks," objected Norma.

"I will go this night to see the reeve and get the right of it. The gentleman chose my brand, but I sell mine own oxen, not the bailiff."

When he was ready to go, he looked to John. "Tis time ye knew y'r ways in the world. Are you coming?"

"Aye," said John.

His mother looked at him. "What you hear this night is not for gossip," she commanded.

John looked at her, reading the warning in her eyes.

"Nay." He shook his head.

The pair of them were silent as they trudged uphill to the reeve's house. John had never called there and was impressed with the neatness of the building and the croft.

The thatch was neat, if patched in places. The building was higher than theirs but the windows were on the level of their own. A holly hedge surrounded a well kept garden with the fruit trees at the bottom. The yard itself was tidy and clean.

Alison, with a wisket of eggs hip slung, was crossing the

yard to the house. She eyed them both in her cool manner but spoke to the father.

"Good e'en Master Jacob. Thy pleasure?"

"To see the good Master Reeve. If it pleases you."

"Will ye come in then?"

"Nay," said Jacob."'Tis a pleasant evening to enjoy the view."

"Oh....Aye" She turned and went indoors.

"She understands the ways of men, that lass," admitted Jacob.

The reeve came out, smoothing his smock, his hair shining golden white in the setting sun. His sharp grey eyes looked from father to son and back again. He walked slow and smooth, like a sheepdog gathering some stray ewes, ready for any unexpected move.

"Good e'en to ye, Master Jacob. Tis trouble?" he asked.

"Not of the boy. He but listens."

"And what then?"

"You have the care of many things on the manor," said Jacob. "The men, the work, the buildings, and you have to account to the Auditors in the autumn."

"Aye tis so. A big task these many years," the reeve agreed.

"What I am going to say is between you and me... for the time being, said Jacob." The reeve nodded in agreement. "The bailiff, who hath been here only six months, what of him?" said Jacob.

The reeve who had, as they say, been born before yesterday, glazed his eyes and asked.

"What of him?"

"He has sold ten oxen," stated Jacob.

"And what of that?" asked the reeve.

"They are mine."

"How knowest thou that?" enquired the reeve.

"The gentleman, who came to see them, chose my brand. It is me who sells my own... And then I have the money in my hand."

Young John sensed the tension between the men. He could not see them both at the same time so he watched the reeve. He reminded John of a hawk, hovering, preparing for the stoop. He saw the flicker in the reeve's eyes as he passed his hands through his hair. A trader's feint to disarm the opposition.

"Thou and I are different men, Jacob o' the Marsh," he said. "I was there when ye took that young ox bull for y'r own and I stood by ye when you bargained with the Auditors. Ye took the oxen herd from my keeping and have done me well and fair with the stock for the demesne. What is in thy mind?"

Jacob explained about the overbearing nature of the gentleman, which had riled the independent spirit of a freeman; of the suspicious method of branding the stock and their delivery; and the suspicion of that which could cause trouble both for himself and the reeve.

"In what way?" The reeve sounded surprised.

"If I deliver my brand, he might say that he has paid the Bailiff.. who has had little to do with me. And I will have no redress...if so be it he has not done so." explained Jacob.

"And I?" the reeve asked with caution.

"If I deliver the manor brand... which I can well do, then you will have to argue with the bailiff, on a bargain that you know naught of...on the saying of a gentleman...of whom we know naught."

The reeve said nothing but John could see that he was thinking hard.

"Then it could be said." John's father went on. "That I will have stolen the oxen of the manor for the gentleman...and there is no honour among thieves."

"How much?" The reeve was interested.

"There was no offer made. He said that he had determined the price with the bailiff."

"Ye have always been a fair, if wily, trader Master. What is on y'r mind?" enquired the reeve.

"I had planned to have three plough teams ready for the winter ploughing. One to sell for a price at the market at Newborough. Two to sell to you for the manor...at the same price. I need the money to build me a house, now that we have a girl in the family. You could graze the old oxen on the marsh ready for killing as winter meat, or selling in the market."

"Tis a good plan," agreed the reeve.

"We have until Monday to set things out. Choose five oxen off the demesne to go with five of the manor which graze on the marsh, and drive them down to me," suggested Jacob.

"What then?"

"You could come with John and me and two men from the manor...If the collectors have a bill of sale, then they take the oxen. And you will then know the bailiff's price, and whether all is well...or not. No bill, no sale, and we will bring the cattle home and be as we planned to be....And you cannot be blamed for losing a sale from the manor if we bring them home."

The reeve looked at young John.

"Heed well thy father, young master. He is, most times, nearly honest."

On the way home Jacob told John, "When you sell your cattle, and they give you the money in hand, then you spit upon it to make it your own and put it in y'r purse. Then you take the price of a quart of ale, or a gallon if it warrants it, and give the buyer a drink." His laugh gurgled in his throat.

"Why do we do that?"

"That is luck money. In case they have bought that

which they did not see. Then they can have no come back to you."

It was his way of redeeming the responsibility to his son's education.

After Church on Sunday, Jacob and John collected the five oxen from the manor. They were all broken for work and they drove down without any trouble.

Jacob had asked the reeve which two men he had chosen for the Monday drive.

"Walt and Twin Tam," was the reply.

"Good enough," said Jacob.

Walt son of Colley the Brewer was not much older than John but he had a chest like a barrel. John was looking forward to the day when he could best him at wrestling, but had to admit that it might be a year or two before he had the body for it.

Twin Tam was a weasel faced, slim young man who gave the impression that a puff of wind could blow him over. A second look into his bright staring eyes made most people think again. It was rumoured that his mother had gone awry, trying to make two boys at the same time. And when Tam's brother died at a month old she said that it was an act of God, and tried to do her best for Tam. He was the best runner in the village and, it was said, he had run down a hare one day.

Hare's always run in a circular fashion, keeping to their known paths and resting so often. When Tam had followed the hare and noted its tracks, he bided his time until the hare was resting himself. Then he had cut across to head him off and drive the hare on to a ground that was strange to him. After that it was a relentless pursuit until he finally caught it. Stretched out it was nearly as big as himself, so he put it across his shoulders like a sack of corn. When he reached home he slammed it down on the kitchen floor and lay down beside it and went to sleep.

The feat had been appreciated in the village and the bailiff had turned a blind eye to the poaching.

John knew them both well and they got on fine together and, secretly, they were not averse to having a scrap if it happened to turn out that way.

Monday morning found them pushing through the sludge and marsh deposits to the Strine.

Jacob led the way on a pony while the reeve brought up the rear on his. The other three, with the help of their staffs and prodigious swearing, managed as best they could on foot, the peaty soil clinging to their legs. Jacob led them on to the wasteland on the far side of the valley, taking his speed to get there at noon, the appointed time.

"We will graze them at Beau Maris and await the outcome," he had told the others.

They were all handy with stock and were able to forestall any likely trouble, keeping the bullocks bunched and at a steady pace. When they arrived at a suitable spot the riders dismounted to let the ponies and the oxen graze. Opening their scrips the men began consuming their bread and cheese.

"We best tarry here together," said the reeve. "We will catch up on the ale in the town when this task is done."

The noon bell from the Church had scarce rung when four mounted men rode out from the town.

"Well," said Jacob, "we will soon know now."

"They appear more like riding men than oxmen," commented the reeve, a wary note in his voice.

The quartet did look a hard set of men. John was quick to notice the leather jerkins and the poignards hanging at their belts.

"These the oxen?" said the one who looked like the leader. "Then let us have them."

"Hast bill of sale?" asked Jacob.

"Bill of sale?.. for my Lord?..." sneered the rider. "What bill of sale?"

Jacob looked at the reeve.

"No bill. No cattle," said the reeve.

"My lord Bellamy has ordered us to collect these cattle. Dost doubt his word at thy peril?"

The man on the horse and the man on the ground tried to outstare each other while the others watched. The reeve refused to crack, until the mounted man made a sign to the other riders.

Immediately all hell broke loose. Somehow Jacob, who had been standing by his horse, was mounted and swinging a cudgel, which appeared from somewhere. The others, readily prepared for such an emergency had joined in before the riders had time to make up their minds whether to drive off the oxen or deal with the men. The oxen were forgotten in the excitement, as the boys wielded their ox-goads, whose sharp points caused havoc among the riders.

Twin Tam was jumping about, snapping with his goad like a cur at bull baiting time, dodging the ponies fighting feet and pricking at the leather jerkins. The reeve who, in his younger days had practised with the riding men at the manor, was mounted, busy guarding the oxen from being stampeded and matching the movements of the other ponies. He had worn a long vicious knife in expectation of a melee. Brandishing it head high he put his heavier pony in a shoulder charge, that he thought he had forgotten, at the leader's pony. The manoeuvre, not expected from a peasant, caught the leader and his pony unawares as it was driven back on its haunches. Fortunately for the reeve he was wronghanded for a proper assault with his weapon and the rider escaped with a slashed jerkin. There was no telling what would have befallen the reeve if his knife had gone where he meant it.

Walt, who was caught between the riders and the oxen found himself beset by two riders at once but, with a quick overhand quarterstaff sweep of his goad, he managed to disarm one rider even as his poignard cleared its sheath. He dropped his goad and grabbed the reins of the other horse and, ducking underneath its head, managed to drag it off balance.

John, who had been knocked down by a blow from a pony, scrabbled for his goad and, as Walt let the pony go, he came afoot. A quick run forward gave him the position to drive the pointed goad into the haunch of the pony. With a squeal like a mare ridden by a stallion it set off for home.

Meanwhile Jacob was pitting his tough blackthorn cudgel against the stabbing of the leaders dagger. Jacob's farm pony was no match for the footwork of the professional but, at least he evaded being wounded until, with a wild hook, his cudgel connected with an arm and he heard the bone crack.

It was all over soon after that, and the horsemen formed up and left the field to report to their master. In the aftermath of the excitement the five of them looked at each other, surprised at their ability to confront the professionals.

"You did conduct yourself well, young John," said Walt. "Madge would be proud of thee. I shall tell her that you can fight...if not ride her."

He measured John with a kindly eye as he reminded him of the day, long gone, when John's incipient manhood had been in question.

John. realising the intended compliment, said naught but held his goad slantwise as a quarterstaff and clashed it crosswise with Walt's, in an unspoken sign that bound them together, in peace and in strife, for years to come. Then they turned to regroup the oxen.

"Master Reeve," said Jacob. "Will you seek the Constable and put the matter to him while we drive the herd over the bridge to the pinfold at Chetwynd End."

It took them about an hour to get the oxen there. Most of the time was spent arguing with the keeper of the toll gate as they had to go through it to cross the bridge, until the Constable arrived and decided matters.

John was standing guard at the fold with his father when a gentleman came up to them.

"Having some trouble Master Jacob of Edgmond?"

"Nay Master Trimlow. Nothing we cannot handle....when we have the right of it."

"There is not much profit in showing spirit against a Lord....even if you are in the right." He had obviously heard the story.

John felt a thrill as he listened to his father.

"I am a free man, as you well know master Trimlow. No serf to be down trodden," stated Jacob.

"Aye. And the cattle?" asked Master Trimlow. in an off-hand sort of way.

"They do bear the Edgmond brand. Although I have the rearing of them. Master Reeve rests in the Bridge Inn while he takes his repast," was the reply.

Master Trimlow. tapped his stick against his leather thigh boot. John noticed that he had not looked direct at his father or himself, but he had run a quick eye over the cattle.

"Aye. Tis so then." He seemed to be talking into the distance.

As he turned on his heel and left them they heard him say.

"It is hard for a so called rich man to go through the eye of a needle."

"Father, who is Master Trimlow.?" asked John.

"He buys and sells meat for the town of Wolfram."

"What did he mean?" John enquired.

"He spoke in Bible parables and, therefore, cannot be blamed for slander. But he meant that we are in the right," was the explanation.

Soon after, Walt and Twin Tam appeared.

"Ye can take your repast the while Tam and I take guard." Walt told them. "Something is afoot with the Reeve and Master Trimlow."

John was tired from the excitement. But not too tired to take his share of ale in the Inn and sit thinking of the happenings of the day. He was sure that his father had purposely involved him in the events, but knew that he would expect him to learn his own lesson without explanations.

The upshot was that Jacob and the reeve stayed in Newborough while other men came to tend the oxen. John, and the other two, full of ale, stumbled home up Cheney Hill. Tam kept them happy singing ballads with Walt, in his deep voice, giving them some of the Tavern songs. John did not understand many of the hints in the songs but he laughed with the other two.

John never saw the oxen again, they did not reappear on the farm. One day he asked his father what had happened to them.

"Your guess is as good as mine," laughed Jacob. "There was no backlash from the bailiff."

John remembered the counsel of his mother.

"Least said soonest mended."

Jacob was well aware of the effect on him when Norma's brothers had gone to Cambridge College. He felt quietly proud of his own physical ability to pursue his ambitions. But they had a standing in the community which even his ownership of land would not allow. 'They toil not, neither do they spin,' as Gill had said long ago.

Norma did not appear proud of her brother's success, but accepted it as if that was the natural way of it.

"They will return to Newborough and tell us the way of the law and merchandise," she had told him. "Mayhap some day you will have need of them."

Father Alleyn had lived over the usual life expectancy of the times and looked as if he was a permanent member of the manor. Only his wife was allowed to see that his normal introvert manner had intensified to a deep disquiet of the future.

"I do not like these changes," he said to her one night.

"What changes?"

"There is talk of the estates breaking up, of people like Jacob taking parts of them for their own use, of a rising of lawlessness in the towns, and in the countryside as well."

"It does not affect us here."

"It will...it will...and it is not a thing that I wish to be a part of. The boys will be more suited to the new order when they return from College."

It worried her to see him gradually sinking into the depression, although she knew that he was still able, on the estate, to command the respect and obedience that he had always been given. Nevertheless she wrote to the sons at Cambridge to warn them.

It happened sooner than they expected.

It was a wet summer, the misty rain blotting out the valley for days on end, seeping into the houses and turning the walkways to ankle deep mud. Alleyn's cough started as a crickle in his throat and developed into a phlegm on the chest that was hard to shift.

In spite of the decoctions of wake robin made by

Mistress Agnes, Alleyn grew steadily worse and the Surgeon from Newborough was called. His prescription of a fine clay poultice on the chest was of no avail and his patient sank into a lethargy which was only belied by his bright eyes. Fortunately young Alleyn was home on vacation, which was a strength to his mother and a means of carrying out the instructions of his father.

As the corn harvest approached it was evident that the grim reaper whose name is Death was calling for his father with his sickle keen. A message was sent to Pierre who had gone to London. He arrived post-haste in time for a few last words before Alleyn the Clerk surrendered to the end which comes to everyone.

It was all new to John, and one day they all went to Church and a great company followed the coffin to the burial ground. He found himself walking beside his mother and his two uncles and stood beside the grave, while his father followed behind.

"You are my son," his mother told him, "my firstborn and the first grandchild. It is your place before your father. He is but married into the family."

His mother walked very straight at the churchyard and did not cry like the other women.

CHAPTER FOURTEEN

After the ceremony the family retired to the house accompanied by the Steward and the Solicitor. They had a glass of wine and the Solicitor prepared to read the Will, while a maid took John and Dickon into the kitchen. Jacob stayed by Norma's side.

The legal gentleman began. "The late Master Alleyn, whose departure we all regret, did in his forethought prepare for this day, in accordance with the Lord of the Manor, and the Steward, and did instruct me as follows.....I will dispense with the necessary legal phraseology.

"Master Alleyn, as you now are. It was your father's wish that you determine with the Steward your future. It was his desire, as you both agreed with the Steward, that you take the position lately held by him, to keep it as he did, following the advice which he, over the years, gave to you, and using your own judgement, with the Steward, for any modifications that the changes in the Nation may make advisable.

"Master Pierre, it was his wish that you make arrangements with the Steward as to your future. It was his agreement, as you have suggested to me, that you buy your manumission, with the stipulation, that whatever you do it may be of a help at some time to the other members of the family, and the Estate also.

"Master Roger. It was your father's wish that, in view of the fact that your sister Norma is now married and has a place of her own, that the local custom of inheritance be amended in this instance. And it was his wish that, as the youngest son, you will inherit any land that pertains to your father, and be responsible for any dues that may be liable to the manor by Heriot. It was his wish that you build a solar to the house you inherit, to be used as a dower for your mother as long as she doth live.

"Mistress Norma. As you are now married, your father doth leave you £50 to be held in trust by you, and used for the education and welfare of the children of your body. Also another £50 to be shared with Jacob, paid by Roger as and when he can, from the profits of the farm.

"The money and the chattels in the house will be disposed of in accordance with the attached inventory.

"Those are his instructions, made in sound mind, in my presence, and witnessed accordingly by Richard de Chetwynde, Jon Dros of Pulesdon and Jordan Brond."

So said Nicholas, Clerk of the town of Newborough, and waited for the reactions of the gathering.

The Steward was the first to speak, "Alleyn, as you know, you are technically bound to the Manor and, for reason's of expediency, I will require to hold you to it. Especially in accordance with your father's request that you replace him on the Manor. It is as well for you all to know, although it is not a matter of gossip, that the future of the Estate is in the hands of God, as to how long our present Master is with us, or to whom the estate may go or indeed, their wishes in the matter."

Alleyn nodded. "It is as my father said, and I would concur with his wishes as indeed I had long counted on it."

"It is well. Pierre how say you?"

"It has been my wish that I should go to London to the firm of a friend whom I met in Cambridge and study Law. We may, with your leave, discuss my manumission."

"It is well...Roger?"

Roger considered it for a moment. "Begging your pardon my Lord, I should wish to discuss the matter with you and Alleyn as to renting enough land to make it sufficient for me and my family, if I marry. And take into account my manumission...if it please you."

"That will require some discussion. But we can arrange that at another time....Now some wine to drink to Alleyn who has gone, and to our future goodwill"

Alleyn's mother rose to call the maid who was waiting with the wine, she would still be mistress of the house until Roger wed. 'I wonder who he will get?' she thought.

Norma had, all her life at home, been used to the role of bystander in all the main discussions. The fact that she was now a married woman in her own house added to her feeling of isolation, and made her keep her own counsel.

Jacob's first thoughts were for his farm and his stock. Nevertheless he was constantly at odds with himself about the conditions in the house that Norma had to contend with. She kept it as clean as she could and never grumbled at the inconveniences compared with the house in which she had been brought up.

As the spring appeared to begin another year, and the first birthday of his daughter came round, he felt the motivation for developing an idea that had niggled in his mind for a long time.

"Tis time to go forward with building a house," he said one evening after supper.

Norma, pleasantly surprised that the matter had come to a head, said, "We could well do with one."

"I have planned it thus." continued Jacob. "The posts and crucks are ready to be pulled into place. The beams are to hand and the rushes for thatching are well dry in the valley ready to be brought. We can find the labour before hay harvest. The bailiff will pay their wages against the oxen which will be ready for his Autumn ploughing."

"And the carpenter?" asked Norma.

"Tis the Fayre in Newborough a week this Monday. I will take the boys to see the gathering while I bargain with Nicholas le Turnour to build the frame. We will have to feed him and sleep him in the house with his apprentice. "

"What of the Fayre father?" asked John.

"Tis held the third Monday in May each year, for selling and buying and some hiring of freemen labour. Twill be of necessity to absent Dickon from school, while the work goes forward."

Monday morning meant an early start and Jacob roused the boys to get the chores done. The morning moon, lying on its back, glimmered through the clouds as they drifted up the valley on the west wind.

"A good day, if it please God," said their father as he looked round, smelling the air. "Tis no great joy tramping in the rain." He picked up the pail and sought the cow for the morning's milking.

John and Dickon, in the half light, set about the tasks allotted by their mother, leaving as little as possible for her to do while they were away for the day.

"Eat well," said Norma when they returned to the house.

"I have packed your scrips with bread and cheese. There will be plenty of ale where you are going, but it's no use spending money on that which we can supply."

She laid out their clean smocks and the boots that they had oiled the previous evening. "You must look your best among the finery of the town."

Dickon was excited. It was his first venture beyond the village.

"Ye saw not the town, John, when we took the oxen," said his father. "Tis a bigger place from Edgmond but only one street. Both of ye keep together. I will allow ye some money but spend it well. Y'r scrip should hold enough food to last ye. And we will meet at the Church door when I have concluded my business."

They set off, up the well known path to the village with the wind at their backs as the day break gave way to the full pleasure of the sun on their faces. When they came to the top road to Newborough John was surprised at the travellers on the way; some chapmen with pack-horses; some peddlers with heavy ox-drawn carts; but many on foot carrying their merchandise . There was a great deal of merriment among the wayfarers, many who seemed to know each other. Jacob set a steady relentless pace that stopped any lingering thoughts of trying to acquaint themselves with their fellow travellers.

The road, cut wide by King Edward's law to protect the travellers from ambush by robbers, gave plenty of room for the ox wagons and peddlers carts and a noisy band of revellers who were telling all and sundry of some great event which was to take place later in the day.

When they came to Cheney Hill and looked across the valley they could see, about a mile away, the square tower of the church rising from the smoke of many house fires. Even so early in the morning they could hear the noise and bustle of the market. John and Dickon were ready to run down the hill to join the throng until Jacob called them back.

"There will be enough excitement ere evening and there be the walk uphill on the way home."

The toll-keeper, and his men, were busy at the town end of the bridge, collecting money and arguing the various tolls. When they were over the causeway Jacob gave each of them half a mark.

"Ye have both served me well this past year. This is thy due, half the wages of a man with keep until you have twelve summers. If ye be asked, ye are not for hiring. I have need of ye....and y'r mother does also."

John and Dickon strolled through the crush, wide eyed at the sights and scenes they had never dreamed of. The clamour of the hucksters carried them up and away until they floated in a sea of noise and turmoil, strange after the quiet of their usual days. The alien current pressed them closer together and caught them up and swept them along, pushing them hither and thither. Strident yells split the crowd as a lumbering ox wagon cleared its steady progress up to the church which rose like an island in the surging torrent.

Allowing themselves to be carried past the Church they came to the open market place. John pulled Dickon to one side as they surveyed the scene. It looked, to the boys, as if the houses had been pushed back for the day, the town shops close shuttered to allow the travelling vendors to rule the town. They had paid their stallage and package to the Manor Executors and were exacting their dues from the milling crowd.

A space, to their right, had been cleared at an alley leading to The Antelope Inn. In it stood a little man holding a mountain of a bear by a chain.

"Come and see the greatest bear of all time," a man was shouting," four pennies each to see this champion. Roll up now. Last chance to see this show."

With that, the bearman led his charge into the Inn yard to where a pole had been set up in front of the ale house. They joined the crowd as it surged forward to tender their pennies to the shouting man. Inside the boys saw the bear fastened to the stake. A man held a dog ready to be unleashed. The boys had seen the bear-dancing in the village but not the baiting. The hound, obviously used to the fray, made a couple of rushes, evading the swipe of the fore claws. On the third challenge it steadied and, as the talons swept past, it ducked underneath and fastened high up on the unguarded flank.

The bearman gave it enough time to make it a spectacle and, with the owner of the dog, went in with a paddle to thrust between the jaws of the dog.

It was enough for the boys. No doubt there would be many wounds on the bear before nightfall and many a dog with a sore head. They went in search of other games.

Further along the street a well dressed gentleman had a stall selling all manner of cures for all manner of ills. Around the stall were many certificates and notices while the stall itself was piled with packages and bottles of aloes and camphor and senna pods and other wondrous cures for all ills, real or imaginary.

As the boys came up to him, he was holding aloft a package and saying, "I have here a powder which will cure all your distempers and ill feelings. Soak it in water and, when you break your fast in the mornings, take it for thirteen days and you will feel full merry and boisterous all the while."

"Rubbish," said a man in the crowd.

The gentleman was taken aback and looked very surprised.

"I always make an offer for those who think that they are dissatisfied with my wares. They may have their money back if they think that what I say is not true."

"Prove it," said the man.

"This man," the gentleman went on, "doth say that my cures are a fake, that my offer to give back the money to customers who think that they are dissatisfied is not true. To prove him in error, friends, I have here one golden sovereign of the realm."

He took it from his purse and held it aloft in his right hand.

"I shall hold it in one hand and let the scoffer chose the hand. If he chooses aright, then he keeps the golden sovereign and I am disgraced. If he chooses wrong then God is my judge that my wares are honest."

With that he smote his palms together above his head with the sovereign between them and proffered his clenched fists, knuckles first, to his accuser. A great discussion then ensued in the crowd as they counselled the man which hand to chose. The gentleman stood impassive, seemingly sure of the choice.

At last the man smote the left hand. A look of woe came in the face of the gentleman as the crowd fell silent.

"It is a pity," he said as he unfolded his fist and turned it palm upward, showing nothing.

There was a surge in the spectators as one man shouted, "show us the other one."

With a show of quiet deliberation the other hand was opened to show the golden coin.

"And now, good people," he went with a rush. "As I was saying I have here, from the greatest apothecary of all time....."

The boys moved off, mystified. They would have been more mystified if they had seen the disgruntled patient, in the evening, driving the gentleman's wagon to the next port of call.

As they moved down the street, packed with stalls and sweating people, looking at cloths that they had never imagined; and wondering at the scents from incense and musk and myrrh on a stall with a man in some foreign clothes; cinnamon, cloves and ginger, blocks of salt and sugar, spices and healing herbs. In their bewilderment, trying to take everything in, they found themselves surrounded by a band of unkempt youngsters of their own age. As they were jostled by the others, the biggest one of the group tried to cut Dickon's purse strings.

Without a conscious thought, John reacted to the practice that he had had with Walt, and his staff came up in a flashing uppercut between the spread legs of the tousled aggressor. Even as the stifled gasp of agony burst from the knife man, the other end of the staff whirled round in an arc and poll axed him between the eyes.

A silence stunned the crowd as the gang leader went down in a heap, Dickon moving to support his brother's back. The realisation of what he had done flooded through John as he waited for the gang to take its revenge.

Quietly, a wizened little man crabbed his way into the ring, calling orders in a strange tongue. The rest of the gang quickly gathered the wounded boy and dragged him away.

Two little coal black eyes bored up into John's, reading the questioning in them, as to whether to fight or flee.

"Get thee gone," the old man said. "We want no truck with the Pie-Powder Court. Meet me in the Blue Boar in one half of an hour."

With that he vanished, leaving the boys to try and sort things out in their minds. Their escapade was forgotten as a man led a trotting horse down the street, holding its head up and scattering the onlookers.

The food stalls and other suppliers kept them interested for a while. Then they followed a stream of men going into The Fox and Grapes at the corner of Backhouse Lane and into a shed behind the Inn. The excited cries made them push their way inside.

"Come on," said John eagerly. "Tis a cock fight."

Although their mother frowned on it, the boys used to sneak off with a pair of young cockerels when they got the chance. The fight was nearing its end as they entered the pit. The victor, with a secure neck hold, was trailing the victim through the sawdust until they were separated.

The next fight was an anti-climax as the boss bird, with its wings beating, went straight in and up, and brought the spurs down with unerring force on the back of the challenger. When the injured cock broke clear it called it a day and disappeared into the crowd.

The excitement in the crowd heralded the importance of the next two contestants. The boys had never seen such birds, long legged like ostriches, eyes as fierce as Sparrowhawks. The betting in the crowd was fast and furious until the handlers faced the cocks up to each other, teasing and stirring them up.

A quick slashing flurry, as they were unleashed brought no result, and the combatants circled each other, feinting and pecking. Another mauling frenzy sent the feathers flying as the crowd roared them on. But there was still a lot of fighting to do.

Again and again the gladiators went at each other, dancing, swooping, strutting, sometimes stabbing home, sometimes missing, clawing with their razor sharp spurs. They were equally matched and gradually the fierceness ebbed away but, driven on by the cries of the spectators, neither would give in.

Suddenly a lightning, lancing peck and an eye exploded. Blinded in one eye the bird, with its head down, had to accept the furious onslaught of his conqueror. He did not hear the boasting, strident cry of the strutting victor.

"Tis a good thing I bet not," said John as they left the shed. "It would have been a good bout for Shrove Tuesday"

"There are two good ones in the village being fettled for that," said Dickon. "Tis a pity we can't join the other lads for it."

"Tis time we found the Blue Boar." said John.

"Tis down St Mary street," they were told.

They were standing about, outside the Inn, wondering what to do when the old man seemed to appear from nowhere.

"Now, young master," he said, "thou art quick to defend thyself."

"Aye," answered John," we practice often. I meant not to hurt him so."

"He did provoke thee. We be travelling people and must guard against the Watch and Ward who doth ever bedevil us in our goings. Where are you from master?"

"My father is Jacob the Herdsman from Edgmond. He is in town and seeks a carpenter to build us a house."

"Is he well known in Newborough?"

"I think so."

"If any do enquire of thee, then thou must say that it was an accident, that thou didst misread the situation. That ye do not know the boy."

John considered it. He could feel the power of the little man pressuring him.

"Thou knowest not who it was... and thou wilt not see him again this day," reassured the little man.

John made up his mind and nodded. "As you will," he agreed.

The little man smiled, the face of an angel, sincere and untroubled.

"I will remember thee....for good or ill," he said and melted into the passers-by.

Jacob found the boys excited but weary, sitting on the churchyard wall, with their mugs half full of penny ale bought off a huckster's stall.

"I think," said Dickon. "That this may be a life of excitement."

John thought not, the noise and buffeting and sharp dealing of the stall holders were not to his liking.

"Did you see the soldiers?" Asked Dickon. "They look fierce and fear no man."

"What of that old man on the church steps?" John asked his father.

"That is a hermit," was the answer.

"A hermit. What is that?" the boys wanted to know.

"He has the name for being a holy man. He has a licence from the Church officers to live in the Church tower and beg for his living."

"And do no work?" asked Dickon.

Jacob laughed. "He will say a prayer for ye, if ye give him alms. Look at the north side of the tower, there is a slit window. There, looking into his cell. He must not leave there or he will be classed with the vagabonds and other beggars."

"Tis a strange life," John decided.

They finished their ale and stood up.

"I have done my business," said Jacob, "let us be on our way."

The trudge up Cheney Hill lacked the spontaneity of the morning and the boys were hard pressed to keep up with their father. They were pleased, when they arrived home, to find that their mother had milked the cow and fed the stock, but they were too tired to thank her and were soon asleep on their straw mattresses in the corner of the kitchen.

The next morning John told his father about the fight and the old man and the arrangement that they had made.

"Who be these travellers?" his father wanted to know.

"We know not," said John. "They looked a queer lot with a different way of talking among themselves."

"Did we do right?" asked Dickon. "The old man wanted to know if ye were well known in Newborough."

"I suppose so," agreed Jacob. "We will say naught to anyone. And wait the outcome...if anything does come of it."

They did not see the travellers again, although word

came down from the village about this strange band of darkfaced men and women who had passed through.

Maykin, the blacksmith, had a wondrous tale to tell of the men who had shown a great interest in his forge, although they appeared quiet and tongue-tied about where they came from. When he asked their name one of them replied "Smith." Thinking they might be making sport, he asked them to show him. Much to his surprise, one of the younger men retrieved an iron rod from a heap of metal that he had put to one side.

In no time at all the boy had the bellows blasting and one end of the rod, red hot and hammered on the anvil, shaped into a spike. Then he pushed the other end into the forge fire and deftly bent it into a half circle, and turned the end to make a hook. He half smiled to Maykin as he plunged it into the cooling trough and held it up to the accompaniment of a gabble of foreign words from his friends.

Maykin asked "What be this all about?"

One of them explained "He hath made a fire hook for his kettle."

Another one put in "All he do want now is a wife to tend the fire."

There was a laugh at this, until one evil looking lad sneered, "If he can find one."

Immediately the young lad gripped the iron like a spear and shouted in his language. The others spread into a ring to watch the fight while the sneering one held up his right hand in surrender, although his left hand dropped suspiciously near his belt knife.

Maykin acted quickly to save bloodshed and pushed between them. His frame was big enough to hold them both rolled together.

"Hold hard, hold hard!" he yelled.

One of the men pushed forward to pacify the situation.

"They be only young cockerels trying out their spurs, master." he soothed.

The circle closed in, and the men moved off. It was only an afterthought upon Maykin's part, when he told the tale, that nobody had paid for the iron.

The travelling women had gone from door to door leaving many bright eyes looking forward to the joys promised for the days ahead. It was not until sundown, when the chickens normally roost, that it appeared that some of them had forgotten to come home, leaving no trace of their going.

John asked if they had a leader but Walt said that no one seemed to be in charge. They had called into the ale house for a quiet drink. No bother. They had spieled the tale about being poor and homeless and his father, in hospitality, had given them a free round of ale. After they left, two of the drinking pots were missing, although Walt said that he would swear that he never saw any of the men take anything.

Nobody knew where the band had stopped the night and, as the days passed, they were forgotten. Except for some nights when the ale was flowing in the Lamb and the memories were magnified to epic proportions.

It had caused a deal of comment among the villagers, leading to the Parson preaching a sermon about wolves raiding the sheep flocks. However, as nobody was really harmed, they thought that a bit far fetched. A couple of women tried to steal some attention by swearing blind that what they had been told had come true. But one of them was a noted bender of the truth and the other had not divulged beforehand what had been forecast.

CHAPTER FIFTEEN

The organisation for building the house was put in hand. Jacob spelled it out.

"Two yokes of oxen to pull the crucks and end posts into position. Then sledge the bundles of rushes up for thatching and collect the poles from the coppice. Nicholas le Tourner comes next Monday and Will the Woodman from the village will be here the day after tomorrow to square the timbers."

It took John and Dickon two days with the slow oxen to assemble the big trees and the ridge pole while Jacob, with a cart, brought in some of the lighter timber.

On the Monday there was a gathering like a young army. Nicholas the Tourner from Newborough took charge, as was his right. Most of the men were used to rough woodwork but were willing to work under the direction of the expert. Will, the village carpenter took second place to Tourner who eyed the bent oaks for the crucks.

"Take care how you work," he said, "split the bent branches for the crucks so that we can marry them up as splitting images. Some of you square the straight posts for the uprights."

As the adzes swung, the pile of woodchips grew and were carried into a heap against the coming of winter, or the extra cooking that faced Norma in supplying the workers. Some smaller chips were put aside to smoulder, when the time came, to smoke the bacon, or the larger fishes from the meres.

Walt and Twin Tam and Mutchkin were there, fitting in with the others as required. One man, with whom John had

had little to do, was virtually one handed. As a boy his right arm had been broken and badly reset, which left it with little mobility but he had a fair grip for when he had to hold anything. He had, by force of necessity, trained his left hand to be as proficient as his right would have been, and he helped the village Woodman by holding the wood with his bad hand and hammering or chopping with his left. When he was young and virtually one handed he had been called 'Wingie', a name he would bear all his life.

John could see that the carpenter from Newborough was going to be worth his money. He watched him closely as he measured and boned the house corners, using the ridge pole, which was some straight Ash fetched from the higher wasteland at Edgmond to determine the length..

"We will want an upper room at one end," said Jacob. "I have planned enough timber for it. And a smaller loft at the other."

Then the digging of the holes for the corner posts began. The undersoil was mostly gravel and sandstone, mixed with a tough red clay which caused some swearing and changing of stints by the diggers.

"Twill be well drained land, John," said the carpenter. "A good thing when the floor of the house will be the soil. That red clay will set like stone overnight."

John, who was wondering how they were going to lift the big beams into place, was surprised when the shearlegs were raised and, with a pulley and the steady draw of the oxen, Jacob gently coaxed them into position.

"The uprights be set root end uppermost to prevent the damp from rising." Tourner again using his experience.

The join holes had been marked by Tourner and drilled by two of the men with a large T-handled augur. Now it was Wingie's task. As the holes married up to join the timbers, John put the wooden pins in the holes. Wingie, with deft and sure strokes, drove them home.

Fortunately the weather held fair and the men were used to working from dawn to dusk in the summer. Jacob saw his wage bill grow in proportion with the frame, but it was no good worrying. He did his share and they did theirs. The framework, with the rafters and the purlins and the cross beams for the upper room, were in place when the carpenter and his apprentice bade them 'Good e'en'. They departed for Newborough, leaving the kitchen a more commodious place at night.

It was all new and exciting to John. In a society, where everyone had to be capable of putting their hands to any work that was necessary for survival, there were men who had a certain skill for special jobs. John took notice of how the Tourner and the Woodman not only worked together but respected each other's skills. He noticed how his father used the strength of the oxen to save the men's energies and how he had the knack of controlling the lumbering beasts to place their load in the exact spot which was required.

When he helped the plasterer to fill the spaces in the wall timbers he found an other attitude to contend with.

"How do you know the mixture?" he asked Giles the plasterer.

"I just learned it from me father," he was told, as the man flicked a shovelful of lime on the heap and splashed some water on it.

"But how do ye know when tis right?" John persisted.

"I just know," was the laconic answer. "I just watched me father."

His smile told John that he was not going to be told any secrets. So John watched him in the way that the plasterer 'had watched his father'. He was not allowed to use the shovel but, later in life when he tried it, he found that he could make a presentable mix. But not with the seemingly careless ease of the master craftsman.

The Woodman fixed the hazel and willow wattles in place, while some women kilted their kirtle skirts into their belts and trod the plasterer's heap to get a good mix with the addition of hair and cow-dung and cut straw. Then, with forks and shovels they rough placed the layers for Giles to finish off. A layer here to set for a couple of days; and then another there; and back to the first again to build the next layer on top of it..

It was a mucky job. At the beginning, John got as much on himself as he put in the wall but, by watching the others, he found the best and cleanest way to get the job done. However it was not the sort of work that he wanted to do to earn a living, and was content to see it done by experts as Giles trowelled the inside and out to a smooth shining finish. And was well pleased with the extra space when they moved in.

As was Norma. She soon ordered the placing of an iron sheet to make a fire place under one corner where the prevailing wind would suck the smoke through a loose patch in the thatch. The floor had been well watered and thumped hard as it dried and, almost overnight the red clay grew a skin as good as a tile. The places were found for the accumulation of ladles and pans and skillets and earthenware pots. The brewing and baking would still be done in the outhouse.

"Now that we have more room," said Norma. "We could have a fixed table instead of having to put up with the trestle one."

Jacob rubbed his chin, as he calculated the effort of erecting the trestle table against the trouble, and expense, of finding the special wood to build a stronger table.

"In time," he said. "In time. Rome was not built in a day, as you know well know."

Norma laughed. "Aye, but I was not the one who was

in charge of that affair."

On the brow of the hill, where the land sloped down to the water meadows, there was a patch of stony land which Jacob had fenced to use as a paddock for the oxen calves at weaning time. Over the years the heavy grazing had broken down the scrub bushes and the coarse grass. But the surface was littered with stones, both small and large. One year, instead of grazing it, Jacob decided to shut the field up for meadow and found himself with a crop of first class hay suitable for the milk cow's Winter feed. But he was annoyed by the multitude of stones which made the scything and raking difficult.

John had looked long at this field, especially when raking the hay. Growing up on his own, apart from the hours spent in school, he become used to Jacob's quiet nod and acceptance of his work as a sign of success. There was a great deal of his father's quietness in his disposition but it had, however, been a help to him, especially when he left school and had to work for his father on the farm.

"Father," he said one day, after they had carted the hay crop off the intake. "The paddock which we took as intake to graze the suckling oxen. Tis good soil and well dunged now."

"It does make a good hay crop for neat cows which is different from the marsh meadows." his father agreed.

"If it were ploughed it would grow crops. It is well drained for barley."

"Have ye seen the stones?" his father objected. "Twould be the devil's own job to plough."

"Tis possible to cart them off."

"They grow, these stones. Every May there are more year after year." Jacob pointed out.

"It might take some time," pressed John, "but, if we sledge them, we can lay the stones for a fence. We can then claim it as an assart. By my strides I reckon near on five acres."

"By proper strides mayhap near on six," his father laughed.

John, whose legs could stretch somewhat when required, looked shamefaced at being found out.

His father laughed again. "We will tell them five acres." he agreed, "How will you fetch them off?" he asked.

"With the hay sledge, if the ground be dry. Tis within the power of the ox teams...if we load to suit them."

"If we decide not to plough," said Jacob. "It could be better for the hay crop, none the less."

"If ye can spare me from the day work, and I could find some extra time, and God in his goodness, gave us good weather....." John put the tentative proposition and waited for his father to consider it.

His father took his usual time to ponder the matter. John, well hardened to his father's ways, curbed his impatience.

Jacob, governed by an innate cunning, had kept his own ambitious thoughts to himself until the time was right to put them into action. When he found that he had a son, whom he wanted to train in the way of life, he felt compelled to do it by hints and half suggestions and placing John in situations where he had to think his way thought the problem.

His father scratched behind one ear. "I will spare thee from the fallow ploughing," he conceded, "but a word of advice maybe. When ye have surveyed the field, mark it well."

He paused a moment and, using his hands to demonstrate

"Ye must walk here and back, and there and back, and carry the stones to leave the heaps in a line like the hay cocks. Then ye can plan to have the oxen at a yoke and Dickon to prick them. Spare y'r steps to gather the stones, and go steady."

"When do I begin?" asked John, all eagerness.

"When ye be ready." His father steadied him down. "We will graze the aftermath, and ye can do your work while the cattle are there. It will take two crops of hay ere the field is suitable for the plough," he went on in his methodical manner. "Then a crop of winter wheat and a spring graze with sheep to curtail the winter pride."

John had achieved his way...nearly.

"There be one other thing," he said.

"And what be that?" Jacob wanted to know.

"When I have done this thing, we can work it as part of the holding but, when it comes to the inheritance it will be mine."

His father was taken by surprise...and looked it. He rubbed his chin and then scratched his head.

"If ye can do this thing, we will find a way to determine it," he said and walked away to hide the smile of approbation which crinkled his eyes.

It took John longer than he had thought. It took more effort than he had bargained for. It took more determination than he thought he had. As he circled round each heap of stones he was thankful for his father's advice about planning his movements.

It was not until he had several rows of heaps ready for gathering in, and had been refused the oxen twice, that he realised how his father had tricked him. When he faced him with it, Jacob nodded his head.

"When ye consider to do work, then plan it to realise the most repayment for y'r strength. When ye plan work for y'r men labourers, then plan it for yourself."

"In what way?"

"Tis an onerous task that ye have set thyself. Too much for me to ask of ye, or day labour to do it properly. If ye had cleaned the heaps behind ye, thou wouldst have been satisfied, or discomfitted, and the field would have remained unfinished."

"Is that the way of it?" John sounded sceptical.

"Aye. Tis not for a young men like you to have the head of experience." His father showed him. "Now that ye have learned the devious plan, we will pair some young oxen with the old ones to break them to the yoke and Dickon and I will help ye to move the heaps. But we will always leave two rows standing to give ye your goance."

And it was so. They used one yoke in the morning and a fresh one in the afternoon. By that time they were ready for an easier task ere nightfall. During the stone hauling, John had learned a deal about breaking in young animals. He was not to recognise that his father was using the same skill in training him, for his life ahead.

Never-the-less it seemed an unending drag. Sometimes, when his father sensed his despondency, he would say that he needed to have the corn weeded or the headland weeds cutting. These days were like holidays to John.

It was a good dry summer which helped him and, on the hot days, he would retire to the Strine in the evenings to splash about and wash the dusty sweat from his body and ease the ache from his shoulders and limbs.

There were some stones, just peeping through the soil and he had to have a spade to dig them out. That was how he became known as 'John o' the Stones.'

Then it was corn harvest. John found the recompense for his toil in the strength and spring in his arms and legs. He was still not man grown but found that, if called upon, he could have matched any of the villagers. But he was working for some one else and only did his due.

At ploughing time Jacob said. "There is the demesne ploughing that is my duty for the land we use. It is my right to deputise a man and, now that you have grown to y'r strength, will ye do it for me? Dickon can prick for ye."

John thought that his father had a peculiar way of setting a problem. He was not asking a favour. He was paying John the compliment of him being able to do a task in which his father took a pride.

John and Dickon took the oxen, with the plough on a cart, to the Manor on the Monday morning.

Kester, the reeve's son was supervising and set them on. The weather had taken a turn for the worse, with days of wet fogs. John, in the furrow, soon found himself plastered with mud, the mist seeping through the hessian sack draped round his shoulders. They had their morning bait sitting on the headland and, at the close of their day stint of an acre, they cleaned and stabled the oxen at the manor buildings and trudged home.

John did not know what the other villagers did but his mother always insisted that they changed in the old house on mucky days. They went into a gigantic meal in clean clothes and, most evenings, they laid out their mattresses and went to sleep to the music of their mother humming to the big spinning wheel.

When the last furrow was drawn, Kester said to John.

"Are ye coming to the Lamb for y'r Plough Ales?"

John thought that was a good idea and loading the plough on the cart sent Dickon home with the oxen.

Relaxing in the warmth of the Inn after the heavy meal, free from the toil of the stones and the heavy ploughing, John felt the youthful strength rising in him. He matched the other ploughmen, drinks for drinks, and sang the songs with Walt. When they pushed back the trestles and the dancing began he was into it with the rest.

Madge looked sleek and fat, but he felt the tension in her body and her suppleness when she came close against him. It was a night for forgetting the ties of work and servitude and he joined in the jollity with the same verve as he had slaved these last few months.

Feeling his head swimming and his bladder full he went out side to relieve himself. Leaning against a tree he felt Madge's arms come round him.

"What is this thou hast?" she demanded. And then she laughed.

He tore himself away and stumbled off into the darkness. His feet knew the way but his brain was in the storm tossed clouds. One minute the ground was as high as a tree, then the slow roll and the tree tops were at his feet. He stopped a few times, leaning where he could, but it did not steady. His mother had told him of the great storms at sea when the waves drowned the ships. But there was no water here. He remembered her stories of the girls singing to lure the sailors. But Madge had only laughed at him. He wondered what he had missed.

The door of the old house was on an easy latch but the floor came up to meet him as he knelt down.

In the morning, when he awoke, sick and heavy headed, he rolled on his back and tried to remember how he happened to be there. He crawled to his feet and went to douse his head in the cold spring water.

All he could remember was Madge's teasing eyes in the lamplight and her scathing laughter in the darkness.

"Thou hast drowned thy cock in the ale," she had provoked him.

Norma, mainly by her family upbringing, had a more outgoing, and far wider, recognition than Jacob of what the organisation on their holding should be.

"Master," she said to her husband, one wet afternoon when they were working at mending jobs, while sheltering from the rain, "It is time that we discussed the future."

Jacob, finished paring a shape of leather for a boot and matched it to a sole. When he was satisfied he looked at his wife. Her intuition told her that he was assessing her, rather than the statement.

"We have little cash money," she went on, "and there is much needs doing on this land before we have a return."

"The rent be paid in labour," was the answer, "It doth take some time for the oxen yield to repay us...only one in five calves are ours."

"Twas fortunate ye had so many heifer calves when ye first took the cattle," said young John.

His father's face was serene when he answered, "Aye. Very fortunate."

John missed the quick look between his parents.

"We did have a few oxen to sell or kill for meat," added his father.

That was true. Even when they heard of shortages in the Country or poverty in the village, Norma always produced a good table and kept her three men fit and well fed for the work they had to do.

"But no money for when we needed labour," Norma pointed out.

"They were always thankful to take some of their wages in kind," was the answer.

"And now John and Dickon are grown to supply the labour," she suggested.

Jacob accepted that it was more a statement of fact rather than disapproval and he permitted himself to smile.

"And take their wages in kind," he suggested with a chuckle, "as I did at their age."

"That is not as it should be," Norma objected. "Avril

doth stand to inherit what the boys are building up."

That had never occurred to John, although he knew how his father had been placed when he was young. He kept quiet, awaiting the outcome.

"I have given it some thought," said Jacob after a considered silence. "There must be a way to reckon it. The land we use has no determination until we assart and claim it. We pay work rent for the marsh lands and woods, but no agreed boundaries."

"What about the meadows?" asked John.

"We are kept from them until after hay harvest and then are allowed the grazing as a favour. If they were not so wet...and dangerous for sheep...they would be kept from us."

"They are used for sheep after the washing," said John.

"Aye. But only a few days before shearing. The cattle suffer not from the worm and footrot and can use them at any time."

They sat in silence, each examining the problem. Norma had lit the fire and, in her quiet way, she allowed the master to tend it. It was her method of getting what she wanted in the end.

Jacob spent some time smoothing the leather with his tough work worn hands. It was his way of not being hurried into a decision. Then he looked at John.

"One day...soon," he said quietly, "a thought will come into y'r mind about the future...as it came into mine...before your age. I need you here to forward the plans for this land. I know not the future or the outcome of all this. Only, if I see the chances for advancement, I take them. There will always be more than enough food to fill our bellies and more than enough work to fill our days. Your mother and I need thee."

John flushed at the compliment and then, as a shattering thought flashed into his mind, 'the wily old bastard', he dropped his eyes to the fork stale he was shaping. Slowly he laid it on the ground and, when he raised his head, his traders eyes matched those of his father.

"I will take a chance," he said.

CHAPTER SIXTEEN

In the spring following Alleyn's death, Lord Audley died. He had never visited them very often, relying on his Steward to carry out his wishes on the estate and his legal rights in the community. Sometimes he would call as he journeyed between his many manors and the Steward would accommodate him, the Manor House in Newborough being listed as ruinous by this time.

"I cannot foretell what will happen now," the Steward told Alleyn. "I have been thinking that you could be nominated bailiff. You know the demesne land and general estate business. There are many times that I have to be absent on business."

Alleyn was too ambitious to object.

"It will depend on the auditors, I suppose," continued the Steward. "There will have to be an inventory made before the autumn visit but I am waiting for instructions. I can rid myself of the present bailiff and you can take his place."

Alleyn had assumed his father's mantle but, as he had missed most of the estate work during the last four years when he was at college, he found it hard going to plan the day to day work. But he had grown up there, and was as devious as his father had been, and just as outwardly pleasant. He was also of the same generation as Kester and let it be known that he was thinking in terms of recommending the continuation of the family's service. That was mainly because he could sense that Kester was willing to adapt to any other changes that might occur.

Fortunately, the reeve was amenable to the new overseer and gave him the benefit of his guidance. He well knew that his own future, and that of his family, was dependant on his cooperation and it would have been necessary, whether he liked it or not.

Both Alleyn and Roger were still living in the family home with their mother continuing to organise the family. The building of the solar was put in hand. 'Just in case' as their mother said, although there was no immediate prospect of either of the boys marrying.

There had been too many sudden changes, and too soon without due consulation, and only half done. The tension between the two brothers, although masked, was the worst part of the reorganisation, spilling over into the relationship between Jacob and Norma. Alleyn had taken his father's position, after several years away from the estate. Roger had been in continuous contact with the job that the older one was trying to adapt to. It was a difficult time for Norma's mother with two men in the house who were deprived of the mutual control of their father. One in charge of the whole estate and one in his employ, both in a state of servitude to the manor.

The tension in Norma's family was eased somewhat when Alleyn took over the bailiff's position and moved into the accommodation of the manor house. All the estate records were in the office there, where he spent most of his working hours, as his father had done before him. It meant that he had the benefit of the steward's housekeeping arrangements and his visits to the home were more of a business nature.

It gave him a certain status in the village which had a steadying effect on the whole community. Everyone accepted their own level in the organisation, most of them with pride in their own ability, but they had grown up in the feudal system and expected an overall leader, whether they agreed with his ideas or not. It was enough for them that Alleyn had been accepted by the Auditors of the Lord of the manor and they were willing to wait and see how he conducted himself. They gave him the benefit of the respect that they had shown to his father, and it said a great deal for Alleyn that he did not outwardly show the burden that he felt, in living up to his father's reputation.

Roger felt much relieved, having the family house to himself and his mother. He continued to share his time between his own holding and the demesne land as he had done for his father. The feeling of being very much the younger brother that had been emphasised by his father's death was outweighed by his inheritance of the farm, but it was not enough to satisfy his craving for independence. The problem of his marriage was another reason which led him to visit Jacob and Norma again.

"You are a grown man now," Norma had told him, "and have a right to your own desires. The steward can object to your choice of wife, but not if he will allow you to buy your freedom, as is the custom of many today."

"My choice of wife will not say that she will wed me. She makes excuses by the arm length."

"Hath she said no?" asked Jacob.

"Not exactly. Now that my father is dead, that is one of the objections that is no more."

"What else?"

"She doesn't say...except that to be the wife of a free farmer, and near gentry at that, is a burden to bear among the women of the village."

Jacob sat quiet while Norma argued with Roger. He thought that there might be another reason that neither Roger nor Norma could guess. At last he said, "bring her here some Sunday. Let Norma do the reckoning and then we will discuss it with your mother. There is also the question of the land which you desire to settle with Alleyn...besides the question of your wife..”

“Then,” added Norma, “we will be able to put it to the Steward and be in readiness for the Auditors.”

When Roger had seen that Alleyn had settled into his role on the manor, he approached him one day.

“About this extra land?” he asked him.

“I have it in mind. Although I am now the Manor’s man in management, it will behove us to look to our own future and guard our steps.”

“The land that I wish, I have marked in my own mind,” said Roger. “It will mean arable farming and few livestock, so I must needs make sure that I do not overreach myself.”

“What have you in mind?”

“There is some good land, too good for sheep grazing and not big enough to carry a flock and a shepherd, so it will be for the plough. There are those in the village who will work for day wages but I have not the money to pay out before the crops are sold.”

Alleyn thought for a moment. “It is necessary to keep the village in good heart, and the skills therein, and not let the labour move to the town. My labour, tied to the demesne, is not sufficient for the busy times. But I have not the money to keep the free men, when work is scarce. We could, with due regard to our rights, share the free workmen and their wages.”

“It is a thought for the steward,” said Roger.

In due course Roger persuaded Gill to come and visit Norma. She had not intentionally played hard to get, but she was genuinely aware of the standards that she would have to maintain with regard to the women in the village, and especially with Roger’s mother. She was past the usual accepted marriageable age but had refused several attempts to lure her into the bed of a common worker, and had made up her mind to settle for the status of an unmarried cook or housekeeper in a manor house.

That was until Roger arrived on the scene with his persuasive ways. It had caused her many disturbed nights and frustrating days and now here she was, coming to meet, in person, the well known daughter of the late Alleyn le Clerk... and Jacob.

If Norma sensed any tension between Gill and Jacob she assumed that it was part of the problem that had to be discussed. She sent Roger and Jacob off for a walk and that left the two women to acquaint themselves with each other.

"She will make a good wife," said Jacob to Roger. "She hath spent some years in the Caynton Manor House and at the house of Sir Richard. Though not high gentry they do have a way which should suit thee."

"With a hundred and twenty acres I could make a good life and be rid of my commitments to the demesne land. We could do well...and she is above a common worker's wife."

Jacob ignored that and said, "that means rent by cash money."

"Aye, but I could manage that, so long as it is paid after harvest to the Auditors."

"Aye. I would wish it were so for me. With John and Dickon coming to age we will have the land assarted but not the time to pay by labour rent on the demesne, and work our own land as well."

When they reached the door of the house they were greeted by the women's laughter.

"Now what?" said Jacob.

"Come in," said Norma, "all is agreed."

"What?"

"If I can tame a rascal like Jacob, Gill will try the same with his double."

The men looked at each other.

"Tis men who make the changes of our way of working ," said Jacob, "not a revolution of women seeking to act above their station."

"Ask my mother which persons determine these things," said Norma. "We will see her next Sunday."

As it so happened Norma made a point of seeing her mother during the week so that her mother was well prepared for the meeting and, in her down to earth manner, accepted that having the Solar as her own, she could live with this choice of her favourite youngest son.

The various problems which they were discussing made the frustration in Jacob boil up when Norma kept saying that she would have 'a word with Alleyn'.

"Look thee here," he said to her one day. "I did fall out with my brothers...and my father, but I cleared out and made my own way...with thy help," he added.

"So?"

"I suppose we had nothing. So, really there was nothing to squabble about. Thy brothers have everything, so why have they to have differences between them?"

"What differences?"

"Oh, dissemble not. I know when the storms are brewing. Tis naught to do with us, but thou art embroiled also."

"It doesn't affect me."

"Aye it does. I am the man on the outside and can see the way the wind blows. I am still the man who works for the family but I am only the man who fathers the children... who ye will see gets educated. They will be the one for books while I will still the poor old bugger who doth plod behind the oxen. Thou hast thy Gentry speech while I still talk like the peasants."

"Jacob!"

"I'm the boy who had to work for his own brothers, and now I have to work for thine. Tis never been right between thee and me since thy father died. 'I will have words with Alleyn,' you keep saying."

"Well, he is the bailiff."

"And another thing," he disregarded her. "Thy brothers have it all. They have their lives assured, why must they have jealousy between each other and pull thee into their wants?"

"I am not involved. Besides there is nothing to worry about."

"There is enough for thee to visit thy home once a week and come back out of sorts. Thou hast enough sense to know when things are awry."

"Well it was difficult for Alleyn when he was at home, and cooped up with Roger, and had to organise the estate over his brother."

The attempt at a conciliation seemed to spark off an unexpected reaction in Jacob. "Bloody Hell," he exploded. "They be grown men...not dogs falling out over a bone."

"Roger wants to get married, but can't...Alleyn is now the estate bailiff and is bound by the Auditors...they are on different sides of the fence. Well what would you do?"

"I would leave thee out for a start, and let us make sure of our holding...before they mess our lot up."

"They wont upset us."

"Oh no? You are the family. They will guard thee and John. 'I will have words with Alleyn!' How do thee think I feel? I have built this place up, not been given it...in spite of the estate owners and their lackeys. This is my farm and no one will take it from me. And John is my son."

"Jacob. It is not like that. Believe me."

She came to him and they stood. Looking. Jacob a hard

burning flame. Norma pleading, questioning.

"Look," she said. "I don't like it either. I do know what is wrong, but we can only wait. It's all underneath...it hasn't blown up yet. Mother's worried as well, you know."

"I'll blow up someday, I can tell you. I keep asking the reeve to keep me out of Alleyn's way."

"No. No. No. You're the man who keeps his ideas to himself. Keep them now. Jacob..please...for me."

"It is you I am thinking of. If it was not for you, I could leave tomorrow...I am a free man, I can go where I will...and make my own way. In Newborough I could have all the oxen haulage business that I could wish."

"I know, I know. Don't take it so hard. Alleyn thinks that he is the important one. But he is nobody without the likes of you...and Roger. He feels just like you."

"The devil he does?"

"Let him think how he wills. You're both good enough to get your way in spite of him."

"You think so?"

She relaxed into a smile.

"You beat the Auditors, did you not?"

He joined in her laughter.

"Aye. We did so, at that."

"You know what my mother said to me when we married?"

"No."

"You've a hard row to hoe...I need you, Jacob."

Alleyn had made a point of meeting Gill to know what he was letting himself in for in his recommendation to the steward, and also walked the boundaries of Roger's proposed extension to his holding to have his plan ready. He arranged a meeting between them all and the steward, but Jacob contained his impatience and stayed at home with the boys.

They were not to know that the steward had made his own enquiries and was well versed in the proposals before they were made. He put his objections to each of them and considered the answers. When he was satisfied he stated his case.

"The boundaries of the land will have to be determined with the Auditors, and the marriage dues with Sir Richard. Some of the land will be claimed from the waste and can be considered as assarted land. That, you may take as soon as you will. The total will have to be defined and presented to the Auditors in the Autumn. I have other business to attend to and will make a point of seeing the clerks while I am in London."

The business was concluded with a glass of wine.

Word was sent to Sir Richard who came home to see Gill, and put the necessary arrangements in hand for the wedding. It was two great days, with a feast at Tibberton and another at Edgmond.

"Tis a good thing to see Roger settled," said Jacob to Norma and John one evening.

"Yes," she answered, "but he is not out of the wood yet."

"What meanest thou?"

"He has to find seven years income to pay for his manumission, and the labour money as well, before he sees any reward. He's no better off than we were for a start."

"And Pierre?"

Norma laughed. "He married into money. And Alleyn, for all he is tied to the manor is still better off than any of us. In the short term at least. There will be more changes, as the time goes by."

"Now, what do you know?" asked Jacob.

"Nothing for sure," she said. "Gossip goes from mouth

to mouth. What matters, is what is not said. Just listen for that which goes through the air, and be ready to act upon it."

Jacob knew what she meant and just nodded his head.

John felt that he would not get a straight answer to any of the questions that arose in his mind. So, for the time being, he kept his own counsel.

He had his own dreams of the future. But of their fulfilment, he knew not.

CHAPTER SEVENTEEN

Jacob and Norma had been having one of their discussions about their future when she said, "We ought to have a share in the sheepflock."

"Why?" asked Jacob.

"There is a deal of good sheep pasture on the manor waste lands. I hear that the trees are lessening with the sheep grazing the spinneys and clearing the undergrowth. And Adeney, besides, is good sheep land."

"I have no desire for sheep," Jacob pointed out.

"No," she shook her head. "But of the future. There is John growing, and he has been talking to the shepherd. If we say nothing direct to him, but let him think he has his own way, he might take to them. Wool is where the money is, and will be."

"Sheep herding be the task of a serf."

"And oxen?"

"What of oxen?" he asked, and then caught her drift. He laughed quietly in appreciation of this woman who kept surprising him. "A plowman could be a freeman, but a shepherd has always been the tied job of a serf."

"Now you are a freeman and own a herd built from nothing. But you've been tied to them...seven days a week...in all weathers."

He nodded his agreement. "Twas the land that I envied and coveted. The oxen suited the land, and the ploy did suit my desires."

"The land above the marshes is the land to own for the future." she said. "The marshes seem to be drying, and giving us more grazing, but they are dependent on the weather. And still no good for sheep. It behoves us to look to the future."

"Be that as it may," agreed Jacob. "Anyway, I have had a thought. Brock, is a good dog but rough, but I should like to keep his strain, but a little softer...better with you folks. I will have words with Thom."

He waited until it was sheepwashing time before the shearing, and Thom the shepherd brought the flock down to a place specially constructed on the Strine. Jacob went to see him.

"Good Master Jacob, thy pleasure," Thom greeted him.

Jacob had helped him on many occasions, but was now exempt as he had his own holding and no share in the sheep flock.

"Two things," he said, "I wish to breed from my dog and I had a thought of claiming a ewe or two in the flock by the manor custom."

Thom nodded his head. "Wool prices have dropped a shilling a tod this year and it may be a good time to buy. If thou hast a good grain crop the prices for y'r corn should do well this year and might enhance y'r bargain."

"What have ye in the lamb crop this year?"

"I do not buy or sell, but if thou shouldst contract with the bailiff, I can mark some gimmers as thine...and ye can have their wool when they be shorn."

"Tis a thought," agreed Jacob.

"Ye would, of necessity, have to supply labour at washing and shearing...but John do enjoy himself herding."

They looked over to where they were guiding the sheep down to the dip and away from it. It was true John was doing his share with evident interest.

"Aye," said his father, "he hath learned animals with the oxen. Sheep be different."

Thom looked at him in a knowing way. "Every man to

his calling." he said.

Jacob did not want to start an argument, he was there to ask a favour, so he said, "It was the idea of Mistress Norma."

"Just so," said Thom. "And the second," he prompted.

"I would have a pup of my dog's strain. Not so strong. And gentler with the women folk. Have ye a bitch suitable for the purpose."

"I have one that I have kept from having pups for a year or two but I have had thoughts of having one more litter from her. She hath been my best worker with the lambs and all but stays at home now to companion Annis my wife," suggested Thom.

"Tis usual for an old bull and a young cow to produce the best," said Jacob. "Mayhap an old bitch and a young dog could do the same."

Thom laughed. "You do think the way of men," he said. "We eye the young women but naught comes of it...When the time is right for the bitch, I will let ye know of it, and we will give him his chance."

Jacob went to the Alleyn and bargained for six gimmers to be added to the flock. It was his allowance, after the custom of the manor. It cost him some of his corn money, above what he wanted to keep for seed and food, plus the expected wool at shearing time.

When Thom sent word, John took Brock up to him and, when he had found out what was required, Brock carried out his part in the project with enthusiasm. In due course Thom picked out the most likely looking bitch puppy in the litter for Jacob and took his profit from the other siblings.

Norma took charge of the new arrival. When Spider, as she was named for her long legs, was old enough she demonstrated her hereditary instincts for herding, with the geese and barn fowls. She was allowed to go with John and Dickon on their walks, on the strict understanding that they were not to allow her to chase rabbits. Everyone was pleased with the result and Jacob put up with the trouble of shutting her up when she was on heat.

A thought, which might have been developed in John's mind by subtle hints from his mother, led him to seek out Thom the shepherd one day. After some talk of the weather and the sheep he asked him.

"Who will take your place, if you get too old?...and no children to follow."

"I know not," was the answer.

"If I can tend the gimmer ewe flock for you and do the boon work of my father, and help you at lambing time and shearing and dipping, ye could teach me sheep."

He did not say shepherding. He meant sheep, how they live, what made them special.

"I shall speak for thee if it comes to a decision," said Thom after giving it some thought. He knew what was inferred.

Remembering the reeve's words about the time when his father took over the oxen herd, John went to see him.

"Good day, Master Reeve," he greeted him.

"Good day to thee young Master John. Hast aught to say?"

"Aye master, tis the shepherd, Master Thom. He seems hard driven with the increase in his flock."

"What of it?" It sounded as if it should be none of John's business.

"He cannot tend more," agreed John. "But there hath been room for a bigger flock these many years now that some of the trees are disappearing...And there is waste land enough to feed them since before my time." He pointed out.

"The family of Thom have been the shepherds for the manor, since before my time," answered the Reeve. "But happen the tups get more lambs now-a-days than the family beget youngsters to look after them."

"Tis not above a freeman to tend the sheep," suggested John.

"And work for me...and the manor...all the hours that are needed?" The reeve sounded sceptical.

"It could be determined otherwise," countered John.

"Like y'r father and the oxen? But thou wilt inherit the oxen in due course." The reeve made it sound as if that was enough for John.

"Not for many a day, if it please God." John shook his head. "and e'en now the horses are replacing the oxen on the lighter soils. It will be the oxen for meat and the neat cows for milk."

The reeve, who was old in years and experience, looked at the young man and envied him his free standing. In spite of being tied to the manor, he himself, farmed more land, for less money rent, than John and his father. His eldest son, Kester, was being tutored to take over the farm and the reeve's duties, if the Manor so desired it. At the least he would have enough money to farm the family holding in a comfortable state and, one day, buy his amanuensis.

"Kester is in charge of the corn weeding today but tomorrow 'fore noon we will have words to thy future."

John said. "Thank thee, Master Reeve." and went his way.

He was disappointed not to see Alison.

That evening he was plaiting reeds to make a basket while his father was shaping a stale for a fork while Dickon was fretting over a yew branch for a proposed bow. His sister was carding and spinster spinning wool while his mother was working the wheel.

"I had words with the reeve this day," he dropped into the quiet concentration.

His mother's hand stopped the wheel abruptly. His father's hand stopped half-way in a cut. Dickon looked on with a speculative eye.

The silence continued until John said, "we had words about sheep."

"What of sheep?" His father wanted to know.

"The ploughing and ditching and corn growing are needful on a farm. But thou, father, have y'r oxen herd, Dickon does y'r farm work well and truly. We now have our allowance of ewes in the sheep flock to fetch a tidy sum of money. But it be so ordained that we must sell all the sheep that are above our allowance... if the Saints do give us an increase."

"Well?" Jacob shrugged his shoulders.

"There be room for many more sheep on the waste lands... if tended properly," continued John.

"Tis the task of the family of the shepherd to tend the sheep. Tis always been the custom on this manor."

"There be no one in his family to follow Thom," John pointed out.

There was a silence while they thought their own thoughts.

"And what of the oxen?" From his mother.

"If it please Our Lady, father will tend to them for many years to come. Then the time of the oxen will have given way to the horses."

"Tis hard to see that," objected Jacob. ""Mayhap the horses would be faster on the Edgmond light land, but they do need a deal more of good hay than the oxen in the winter time. And the hay from the marshes will clem them."

"Old Thom could tutor me in the way of the sheep," John continued. "As he grows older and is forced to rest himself, I could take the sheep flock...as ye did with the oxen."

"A shepherd's job is the task of a serf," his mother objected.

John hunched his shoulders. "Oxen was the task of a serf," he said looking at his father.

"And what said Master Reeve?" Asked his mother, quickly, to forestall an argument.

"Tomorrow forenoon we will have words with Kester," John answered. "He takes a share of the work from his father the reeve."

"You will have to guard yourself with the Auditors," ventured his mother.

When John approached the reeve's croft next morning, it was as if Alison had been looking out for him.

"Good day, Master John," she said. "My father the Reeve doth await upon thee."

John, feeling in need of support, was embarrassed by her semi-officious manner.

"Nay," she said, the laughter in her eyes. "I did but jest. You do yourself well this day...and for the manor lord. They have talked," she added as she led the way into the house. "Not to me, but I did listen."

"Good day, good masters," said John.

"Sit ye down young John," the reeve invited him.

Kester began the discussion. "The sheep flocks and pig herds have always been the care of serfs. The animals need herding day and night at times. Tis not a task for day labour."

John nodded and waited for the rest of the comments.

"The young of the Thoms were brought up with lambs and know them well," explained the Reeve.

John knew what was meant, second sight between animals and their caretakers. "I know animals. I was reared with oxen. But sheep have been money from when memory was not...and will be until we are no more." The reeve nodded his agreement but kept silent. "Ye have kept the numbers of the sheep to match your shepherd," went on John. "And that which was needed to manure the land for your corn."

"It is as it was when I was made reeve by my lord... and it has always been as he desired. It suited my efforts on the estate. Why must you do more than that which lies to your hand?"

"My father," answered John, "was a landless free man who planned to take the land which all thought useless. When he is gone I plan to inherit what I can, but twill be necessary to have money to rent it...if that be the offer."

The reeve looked at Kester and waited for his reaction. He had stood by John's father, and had not regretted it. Now was the time of the younger men. It was in the nature of their life. The young bulls growing to maturity and bossing the herd. He would give all the help that his experience could supply, but the future was between the two young ones.

At last Kester spoke, as cagey as his dad. "What is on y'r mind?"

"I have had words with Master Thom. He will speak for me. I do some of my father's ploughing for you and the boon harvest. I spend my other time with Master Thom to do y'r day work with the sheep, dagging, washing, shearing and the like."

"That could be ordained...but you will draw an unskilled day wage?" The reeve sounded unbelieving. "I must defend my duty on the mnor."

"And keep my gimmers in the flock and not sell our increase this year," pressed John. "...and draw the fleece money on the count."

"The fleece money is not mine to give upon the

accounts," the reeve objected.

"Thou wilt not be put in jeopardy, I do vouchsafe ye," agreed John.

Alison appeared with a tray and put three jugs on the table. None of the men acknowledged her presence, the three of them, blank faced, keeping their thoughts to themselves. The training of years kept John quiet. He had said his say.

'Enough is as good as a feast.' His mother had said.

'God help those that help themselves.' His father had shown him.

The Reeve picked up his jug and held it head high in acknowledgment.

"The prudent man guards his footsteps." he said and left it at that.

John went away with a sense of impending doom gradually replacing the burning optimism which he had felt when the original plan had entered his mind. He knew that he was strong and skilful, but had he the stamina and, most important, the good luck? He had heard many tales from Newborough of the men who had made quick fortunes and also, of those who had lost them just as quickly.

When John told his parents of the outcome of his talk with the Reeve, Jacob thought that he had reached another milestone on the road to rearing a man. He, himself, knew oxen as well as Thom knew sheep and, while he had tried to guide and instruct John in animal care, he was at a loss on how to advise him on sheep management. Unless he let Thom do it for him.

He was still conscious of the rough upbringing he had from his own father, and how he had been limited from a wider experience on farming matters. His outward reticence towards John was balanced by his discussions with Norma and he often took her advice in his attitude to their son.

He was glad that John had inherited the independence

from him as well as the perseverance to get things done the way that he planned. Also the mental aptitude that he had learned from Norma. But, for Jacob, it was an effort, inherent in all stockmen, of giving to sheep the same dedication, as he did to his oxen.

Nevertheless, he had to admit, that was the day that John had reached his manhood.

EPILOGUE

Mr. Marsh paused, and reached for his tankard and took a drink.

"That's it for this year."

"Aw," they said.

"Never mind. Next time will be the Tale of the Shepherd. When John gets his sheep flock on the land that they had cleared. And gets married."

THE PLOWMAN'S TALE

Jacob o' the Marsh

A lad with a driving ambition who manages, with the aid of medieval customs to rent a piece of land on the Edgmond Manor, marries and begins the family..

THE SHEPHERD'S TALE

John o' the Stones

His son who takes to sheep herding on the land that his father had won, to produce wool which was the main National export and, with the aid of his uncles, buys the flock.

THE SOLDIER'S TALE

Will Graham

A soldier, wounded at the Battle of Shrewsbury, who was befriended by the family. He marries John's daughter and sets up as a Wool Merchant. Buys the produce of the smaller farmers and sells it to the Staplers.

THE SAILOR'S TALE

Willeyn Marsh

The fourth man, son of the soldier. He makes a career on the business that his father had built up', exporting the wool and bringing home goods from the Continent.

GLOSSARY

ASSART. Land that has been cleared and registered with the Manor
ALES. Celebrations at the finish of a communal task e.g. ploughing, shearing, harvesting.
ALL SAINT'S DAY. 1 November, Saxon, Samain. All Gods of the underworld.
ANCELLOR HOUSE. A house used by the Crusaders when in this country.

BEDS. Usually a plaited palliasse laid on the floor and put away during the daytime.
Truckle Bed. Sometimes with a low built wooden framework.
BLOODSHED. Trial for anyone committing a wounding offence.
BOTTLES. Made with leather. As were drinking Jacks.
BUGANS. A wicked spirit.
BOWMEN. Men trained in Archery. Compulsory Sunday afternoon activity.
BILLMEN. Foot soldiers who used any weapon to hand, axes, billhooks, etc., any cutting tool.
BILLHOOK. Used on the farm for coppicing and clearing wood brash.
BUTTS. Where the bowmen practised short term accurate archery.
BIRTHING PILLOW. A soft pillow used when ill or in childbirth instead of the usual wooden roll.

BREAD. A rough ground mixture of wheat and rye with the bran not taken out. See manchet.
BROWIS. A pottage made by pouring boiling water on slices of bread seasoned with pepper and salt, adding a lump of butter and a slice of onion.

CONEYS. Rabbits brought into the country by the Normans.
CHEESE. Made with ewe's milk, after the lambs had been weaned.
CUSTOM of the MANOR. Sometimes the feudal laws were amended on each Manor, to suit the Lord of that Manor.
CLOUT. the distance which was used for the 'long shoot' with the bows. Usually about 200 yards. Training for the barrage to open a battle. Six arrows in the air before the first one lands.
COPSE.COPPICE. A plantation of trees, kept for growing staves etc., These were grown from the roots of the trees which had been cut down and the shoots left to grow.
CRUCKS. Bent tree trunks which were used for the shape of the roof.

DEMESNE LAND. Land used by the Lord of the Manor for his own cultivation.
DEODAN. An object, whether animal or inanimate which had caused the death of a person. Its value was forfeited to the Crown and given to charitable purposes by the Lord of the Manor.
DOUBLETS. An upper body garment for men. Lined, hence 'double'. It was usually belted and had a skirt, shortened by young men and soldiers

to mid-buttock as a matter of fashion.

EASTER. Christian feast to celebrate death and resurrection of Christ.
EMBER DAYS. Special fast days set up by the Church.

FAIRS. Market Days allowed to a town by the King where only the travelling merchants were allowed to sell their wares, after paying their dues. Sometimes used as 'hiring' fairs for servants etc.
FREEMEN. Men who were not bound, by servitude, to a Manor.
FALLOWS. Land which was 'resting' from having a crop. They were ploughed, and cross ploughed to kill the weeds and encourage fertility.
FISH TICKLING. A method of catching fish as they rested in the shadows. A good form of poaching.
FUSTIAN. A strong twilled cotton fabric with little nap.
FLAX. Grown mainly for the strands which were harvested from the stems by soaking and crushing.

GEBURS. Free men who were allowed a house and garden and the tools necessary to work on the Demesne, for day wages. When they died, or left, all their chattels etc., and the tools that they had been given were returned to the Manor. All discrepancies being made good.
GILT. A young female pig which had not had a litter.
GOWN. A lady's upper garment worn by Gentry,

or better class women to show their rank.

HOP-HARLOT. A covering of rough heavy material used by the working classes. Dagswain.
HOSE. Upper hose, joined-together to resemble modern trousers. Originally worn separate as in general modern stockings.
HOOK and by CROOK. Allowance of wood for householders. Hook, loose wood on the ground; Crook , what could be pulled off the tree. Scot wood, an allowance from the manor for repairs to the houses.
HUE and CRY. Any person wishing to make an arrest could call for help in doing so. Everyone was obliged to join in but whoever started it without due cause was liable to be punished.

IN-TAKE. Small field near the house. Taken from the waste land.

KIRTLE. Long female outer garment with sleeves which were laced from the elbow to the wrist so that they could be rolled up when working.

LEATHER. Animal skin, rubbed clean of hair or wool and cured. Tanned professionally or soft tanned at home. Sheepskins sometimes split to provide parchments for writing. Some times processed to provide a substitute for chamois leather worn by knights under their armour. Also scrubbed to give a translucent coverings for window spaces.
LEYWRITE A fine from the Lord of the Manor

for any woman giving sexual favours.
LAMMAS. 1st August. Saxon, Lughnasa. First fruits Festival.
LINEN. From the strands of the Flax plant. Sometimes grown as a stand in the gardens or small plot.

MERCHAT. A fine to the Lord of the Manor for a daughter to marry without the Lord's consent, or when leaving the Manor. Half a ploughman's annual age.
MID SUMMER'S DAY. Saxon Summer Solstice.
MAY DAY. 1st May. The Saxon, Beltain. Never regarded as a Christian Festival.
MALT. Used in Brewing. Made by sprouting corn and then killing it by heat and grinding. Mainly Barley but also Oats.
MARTINMASS. 11th November. The time when beef was killed and salted or smoked for winter use.

NEAT COW. Female ox kept for breeding and supply of milk.

OX. An male which had been castrated at birth.

PALLIASSE. Plaited straw bed laid on the floor. Put away during the day.
PLATES. Wooden. Carved and polished from a beech ring.
PENNY ALE. Lightly brewed ale used for women and children.
POACHING. Taking any animal belonging to

the Lord of the Manor without permission. Rabbits in a warren and hares. All game birds and animals.

REEVE. Originally a man appointed yearly by the workers to act as foreman. Later, if suitable, the manor Lord could make him permanent and sometimes, it ran in the family. Always at the wish of the Lord.

SERFS. One who was owned by the Lord of the Manor and governed by the Customs of that Manor.
SNARE. A sliding wire noose set at the head height on a run favoured by a rabbit etc.,
STAPLER. A licensed Wool Merchant. Bought and sold in the markets in the Government regulated Staple Towns. e.g. Shrewsbury.

TRENCHER. A shaped slab of un-leavened bread. Used as a plate at mealtimes, and then eaten when softened by the gravy.
TOURNAMENTS. Held by the Knights as a means of keeping them fit for battle and entertainment.

VESPERS Anglican Evensong.

WATTLE and DAUB. The means of in-filling the wooden frames of a house before the use of bricks. See house building in text.
WATCH and WARD. Policing towns. Watch in charge during night hours, Ward through the day.
WORKMAN. Usually referred to the proficiency

required in the actual work.

WARREN. The series of tunnels used by rabbits. They were fenced originally by the Manor. Right of warren was the grant to the Lord of the Manor to appropriate any waste land for the purpose. Hence taking any rabbits, although running free, was poaching.